MW01143010

WAR EAGLE WOMEN

TINA COLEMAN BAUSINGER

To Marilyn

SMP

SOUL MATE PUBLISHING

New York

WAR EAGLE WOMEN

Copyright©2013

TINA COLEMAN BAUSINGER

Cover Design by Rae Monet, Inc.

Published in the United States of America by
Soul Mate Publishing
P.O. Box 24
Macedon, New York, 14502

ISBN: 978-1-61935-587-3
eBook ISBN: 978-1-61935-306-0

www.SoulMatePublishing.com

Acknowledgements

The writing and publishing of War Eagle Women has been such a wonderful, terrible, horrifying, fantastic roller coaster ride. It began as a small seed, a kernel of a question: "What if a nurse, working in the surgical ICU, was on duty the night when her daughter was brought in severely injured, and not expected to live? What could have happened that the nurse didn't know her daughter was in trouble? What greater question about daughters and mothers, the fragile bond between them, could be asked? The idea of a secret not belonging to just one person emerged. Then the question became, "What would we risk to keep our secrets?" Or, even more intriguing, "Do we really keep our secrets, or do they keep us?"

This book would have never happened if I had not met Traci Borum, a dear friend and teacher of creative writing at Tyler Junior College. It was because of your wonderful, addicting class this story began. Your insight has been invaluable, and your friendship a treasure.

Linda Gary, Ph. D. is also an important force behind this novel, because you took a few minutes out of your crazy schedule to encourage me, a 36-year-old non-traditional student working a 40-hour week and going to school as well, that, yes, I could write and should not stop writing until something was published. You made me feel as if it were possible. For that, I will always be grateful. I want to be like you when I grow up.

To Brinda Carey, Joy Keeney, and Sandi Johnson who read different drafts and gave invaluable feedback, I am so very thankful. Y'all are my heroines. Joy, I have known you for longer than I have known my husband, and my life is richer because of you. Brinda, you are one of the strongest, yet kindest, women I know, and I admire you very much. Aunt Sandi, thank you for believing in me.

To Mary Stone and Jennifer Booth, who answered my hundreds of nursing/hospital related questions because I wanted my book to sound authentic, I thank you. Jennifer, you are indeed a rare find of a friend, and I am so happy to have met you.

I thank the my own great-grandmother, Ella Mae Trout, who is something of a legend in her own right, who got me thinking about those wild Cherokee-Irish people who inhabit those mountains, and who they might have been. Grandma Ella Mae, I always think of you when I hear the legend of Sequadee and War Eagle. May your wild spirit rest.

I also thank my patient Lee, who listened to every painstaking detail, and even gave me some ideas when I was stuck. Lee, you are my Henry. I hope you see yourself in him. Nathan, Sarah, and Jordanne, you are my heart and my song. I love you dearly and am so glad that, for a short time, God entrusted you to me. I'm the luckiest mom alive. Dad, I haven't forgotten you. I love you and hope you are proud of me. Rest in peace.

Chapter 1

EDEN

There are some days I'll never forget.

My first day of school. My first kiss.

The day I met my daughters' father.

The day my babies were born.

But more than all of those days, the day I'll never forget will always be *that* day, the day Samantha lingered on the fence between this life and the next, trying to decide which side to choose.

I sat there at her bedside, and willed her, begged her, cried out to God, Buddha, or the Devil if he was listening, to bring her back to the world of the living. I would have sold my soul if it meant she would be laughing again, or even yelling again. Mama always told me, "What goes around comes around, and the Devil gets his due!" I always hated when she said hillbilly crap like that. *But, oh God, please don't take my daughter because of the things I have done. I can't bear it.*

It was funny how little things seemed unimportant until a tragedy transformed mundane into unforgettable. That morning, she ate Cheerios at the table while listening to her iPod too loudly. I griped at her to turn it down, and she pretended not to hear. When I walked over to turn it down for her, she absentmindedly twiddled a lock of her auburn hair with her index finger, something she hadn't done since she was a baby. It touched me so I left her iPod alone, even though I couldn't stand that music she'd started listened to.

She didn't know that when I went back to the stove I studied her from behind as she poured the syrup on her pancake, making a smiley face like she always did. It made my eyes tear up because it gave me hope that somewhere, deep down in her core, my sweet Sammy was still inside the stranger she'd become.

Twelve Hours Earlier

The thing I've always remembered about that night was the rain. Every television in the unit, muted for the patients' consideration, was turned to the weather. The news was the same on every channel. I watched live footage of the creek creeping up under the one-lane bridge, just inches away from spilling over. Words and figures flowed across the screen, spelling out statistics from the last five times we had flooding like that in War Eagle. The news anchors, faces grave, explained that the last time the river flooded, there had been 199 fatalities. That was about ten percent of our population then.

Great sheets of water pounded the windows, and deafening thunder boomed throughout the hospital. More than once, the power failed, and the lights flickered off.

The emergency generator hummed, then reset all the ventilators and monitors within seconds. A burnt mechanical smell lingered in the air. Thankfully our apartment wasn't close to the creek, but Nana's house was, and I worried about her. She refused to leave, no matter how many times she'd been told. She barked, "If after all I've been through, that old river tries to take me, then I reckon it's time. That river and I are sisters, and we understand each other."

I was so tired and having trouble concentrating on my assessment sheets. I decided to drink some of what passed for coffee around there and tried to clear my head. I had been working the night shift at the Surgical ICU for five years, but sometimes it felt like longer. I still didn't sleep well, and was tired most nights at work. I took my coffee wandered over to the window. The rain just wouldn't let up. It had been busy at work that night; too many accidents, too many family disputes ending in violence, too many people getting hurt.

I jolted from my reverie when the charge nurse hung up the phone and told Jennifer, the nurse next to me, that she was getting a patient. A "Jane Doe," (a term we used to mean an unidentified female) approximately sixteen or seventeen years old. Her family hadn't been located yet. She had been in a head-on automobile collision- the vehicle she was riding in totaled beyond recognition. The driver, barely alive, would be my patient. If he made it to the hospital at all, his surgery would be extensive and risky. Both patients remained in serious condition. When the trauma surgeon was finished, the girl would come to the ICU while they decided if she was stable enough for the neurosurgery she would undoubtedly need.

I helped Jennifer get her room ready. We turned the blankets down on the bed, got a bath kit, and located the paperwork. We silently worked together, like dance partners in a familiar waltz. Jennifer, my favorite nurse to work with, was knowledgeable, kind, and had a wicked sense of humor that often made me laugh until my sides ached. What I loved most about her was her compassion for those she took care of. I knew that many mornings, her thoughts rested on them so that she couldn't sleep during the day.

I was pouring another cup of coffee when the ER nurses brought the patient in. They talked busily back and forth to themselves and in worried tones to Jennifer. "Still waiting on results on blunt trauma labs, drugs of abuse, and alcohol screen. Still need an ultrasound of the abdomen and MRI of the C-spine, but she's already had the head CT. She does have a minor head hematoma. She's got a crappy H&H so we have given her two units of blood, and she has an order for two more, plus two units of FFP's and a ten pack of platelets. Neurosurgery's been consulted. She'll probably have to go to the O.R. soon. OB has also been consulted, because she's about nine weeks pregnant."

As they wheeled the patient past the nurses' station and into the open room, I saw a flash of matted red hair covered in blood. Even though I couldn't see the patient's face, I didn't have to.

A mother knows her child.

The coffee pot fell from my hand and shattered by my feet. I didn't feel the burning liquid as it puddled around my shoes.

ELIZABETH

There used to be nothing I liked better when I was a kid than to wake up to the sunrise that surrounded our little cabin in the Boston Mountains. On a chilly autumn morning, fog rested on the surface, like so many heavenly clouds. Most people had never heard of my mountains. If they asked me, which they didn't, I would tell them that my cabin sat high on the white limestone cliffs on the War Eagle River, but they didn't know where that was either. I liked it that way.

My grandma, a full-blood Cherokee Indian, believed those limestone bluffs held the spirits of those who had passed on from this world. That, somehow, the pain and sorrow from the past remained trapped in those bone-white cliffs. "Remember, Elizabeth," she would say in her broken Cherokee accent, "we are War Eagle Women, descended from the first female warriors. We do not break. When we die, our spirits return to these cliffs, to this river, to rest and wait for our time to help future generations when they need us."

I believed that.

Sometimes when I stood on the banks of the river, the cool breeze on my face, I could feel the souls of those who had died in those wild waters. One spirit in particular haunted me, probably because I was the one that put him there.

My grandma used to tell me about our ancestors, the first War Eagle Women. If I thought about it, I could picture her face, dark and beautiful, and her hands, both strong and feminine, her long soft fingers braiding my hair as she spoke, sometimes so softly I'd hold my breath to hear.

"Once upon a time, there was a strong tribe of Cherokee who lived here on this mountain. The women were from the river goddess, the men from the cliff gods. Together, they were strong, even though they were small in number."

Her fingers stopped braiding, and I knew she was lost in thought so I waited. Soon she started again, her fingers weaving my hair without her even looking.

"One day, the young warriors were called to battle. The women were left alone with the children. The warriors were slaughtered by the other tribe, a tribe of Choctaw. They killed all of our husbands, all of our brothers. They rode their horses slowly, so full of pride. The scalps of our men were strewn across their horses' backs, our men's blood trailing the ground behind them. The Choctaw men laughed when they saw us. Their eyes burned with lust and their hands reached with greed to take what was ours.

"But we, the War Eagle Women, were not like the women of the other tribes. Our mothers, our fathers, taught us the same skills as the braves. We could cook and sew, yes. We could chew the leather of a calf to make it soft for moccasins and cook soft bread on the fire, yes. But we were also taught archery and how to ride a horse. We learned how to make the arrow tips so sharp they cut a man to the heart.

"The Choctaw were surprised when their most highly decorated warrior bled from our arrows. We frightened them with our battle cry. The river heard us and caused a storm to come from nowhere, blurring the men's vision. Some of us stood on the top of the cliff, watching their descent into the river. We stoned them all, and the river helped us, by licking their bodies up in her waves and pulling them to her iron belly. Those men did not know the power of the War Eagle Women. Now they do."

My grandmother would always take a single feather and weave it in my dark brown hair that looked like hers. She said the feather would keep me from harm, because it was her protection, passed down from the River Goddess. Kids at school laughed, but I kept it. Even if they were the lowest of the white trash mountain people, they still looked down upon us who had Indian blood. Pa's strong Irish genes showed in my skin color and lightened my hair some, but it was still written in my DNA that I was a Cherokee. I couldn't hide it even if I wanted to. By the time Samantha came around though, the Irish genes had all but washed away the evidence of the Indian blood within her, except her wild spirit.

I believed Grandma's stories about the War Eagle Women. Sometimes, I still hear her within me. I feel her spirit. When she comes, it is usually to warn me of something that is to come.

She appeared to me in my dreams every night for two weeks. I usually woke up feeling anxious, a feeling of foreboding stealing my sleep and my peace. My granddaughter, Samantha, was on my mind. Not just because of her seventeenth birthday. It was something else. Something was going on with that child, and I couldn't put a finger on it. She had restlessness in her spirit. I wished she would have talked to me like she used to.

I could still remember when Samantha was born. Eden labored for twenty-seven hours long, and the doctor nearly went in and took her. When Eden handed her to me, she was so weak from childbirth she could hardly smile. Her reddish-brown hair stuck to her face. Her brow was gritty with sweat, her eyes bloodshot and tired, yet she beamed with the joy of it all. I sat in the rocking chair and held tiny Samantha in my arms. We told each other our secrets, even back then. That child was more a part of me than her mother ever was.

I dreamed Samantha was lost and crying out to me. She held her hand out and I tried to grasp it, but I couldn't. I saw her fall from the cliffs, her strawberry-blond hair floating in the greenish water.

I saw the storm clouds gather, but was powerless to stop them.

As I looked in the bathroom mirror, I didn't even recognize the stranger there. My white hair thinned and my skin sagged from the effort of trying to keep this soul inside. I didn't really feel like that was me in the mirror, but some cold imposter, a ghost.

I'd been sitting outside on my porch with my book of poetry when Emily called me about Sam's accident. My heart leapt in my throat, and my hands shook unsteadily. God only knew how Eden was holding up. I climbed up in my old Jeep and sped down the dirt road that led to the highway.

My wiper blades could hardly keep up with all the rain and the inside of my window kept fogging up. I approached the bridge and saw with horror the brown water foaming with rage, spilling across the road, possessing the bridge. I felt more than saw my way across. It really didn't matter. I could find my way down that road in the dark. In fact, many times I had found my way out of places nobody else thought I would. Like the day I killed my father.

SAMANTHA

I sank onto the overstuffed leather sofa, tired and slightly drunk from playing quarters with a couple of friends (okay, so calling them friends was a stretch), from school. At last count, I had downed two beers, two shots of tequila, a shot of vodka, and I was starting to feel sick.

I found my way up the fancy spiral stairway to the bathroom. I closed and locked the door and immediately started throwing up. The vomit kept coming and coming, with no end in sight. I rested my face for a moment on the cool, decorative tile. What it must be like to live in a place like that: a place of tennis partners and trust funds, a new Mercedes for your birthday and a promised Harvard education. But that's really fine. I didn't want to go to Harvard. I never wanted Harvard.

I collected myself enough to stand up then washed my face at the antique basin. I put my mouth under the faucet and rinsed the puke out of my mouth. I stared at my reflection in the mirror. I appeared pale, like I hadn't slept for days. That made sense, because I hadn't. My eyes were reddened from the alcohol that still coursed through my veins. My head was pounding.

I opened up the medicine cabinet above the sink, hoping to find a few Tylenol. Man, these people were druggies! The stash downstairs on the coffee table had nothing on what was stored here.

Vicodin, Codeine, Phenergan? What was that last one, anyway? I guessed if you had the kind of money these people did, you could buy anything. I popped a pill into my mouth, and washed it down with more water from the faucet. I got ready to close the medicine cabinet and something caught my eye. A stack of razor blades.

Expertly, I removed one from the case. The sharp-edged metal gleamed in the soft lighting of the bathroom. Slowly, I sat down on the toilet, still holding it.

My long sleeves concealed the evidence of my expertise. Tiny scars danced around my forearms. I knew I shouldn't, but the cutting helped somehow convinced me I was still alive. I could feel something other than the pain. Plus, when the blood came, it felt like a little of the pain went away. At least for a while. At least, I felt something other than the creeping numbness that threatened to steal my very sanity.

How easy it would have been to finish it there. It would have been a while before anyone found me. I began filling the old-fashioned claw-footed bathtub with warm water. I was startled by someone pounding at the door, but they moved on. There were three other bathrooms on that floor, and three downstairs. They'd find somewhere else to go.

When I decided to do it, I wouldn't plan on messing around with "a cry for help." No, I would slash myself vertically and deeply, until my arm from wrist to elbow was reddened like the Nile. I wanted to leave nothing to chance. I heard somebody making noise at the door.

"Go away!" I yelled in my most menacing voice. But they weren't listening. I dropped the razor blade into the small trashcan on my way out.

Where is Matt? I pushed my copper hair out of my eyes and searched around the crowded, smoky room. Somebody had turned the speakers up all the way and the bass seemed to be thumping right through my head. There was a couple next to me on the couch making out. I wondered absently how long they had been there. I couldn't remember the events that led up to showing up at that party. I didn't even know the girl who hosted it.

A big bowl of assorted pills sat on the antique coffee table. To get into the party, I had to bring some pills. I stole some of my mom's leftover pills from when she had surgery. Mom would never know I took them, that was for sure.

I tried to stand up and find Matt, but suddenly my legs wouldn't work. I laughed at myself. *I'm so pathetic.* Mom would have been in shock if she had known what I had done. I would have been in so much trouble. She also would not have approved of the ensemble I'd put together: short black mini, black fishnets, a low, scalloped top, and a ton of bracelets. Mom hadn't noticed that I had gotten another hole in my left earlobe. A couple of days earlier I had decided to dye my hair black. I bought the hair dye but hadn't gotten the guts to do it. I was just sick of having the same long red hair as my sister, and my mom… I was not the same as them.

Matt came over and tried to hand me a drink.

God, no. I shook my head.

"Well, ya ready to go then?" Matt exhaled, and dropped his cigarette butt into an abandoned drink on the coffee table. He gulped the drink he had brought to me. "This party sucks," he grumbled.

Matt Pierson was not hard on the eyes. Tall and muscular from lifting weights every day, he wasn't the least bit modest either. With his dark hair and goatee, he appeared like sort of a mix between rock band and punk. Together, we made a pretty good couple. Everybody said so. I was tall, lean, long-legged, and had the trademark O'Neill eyes. Although my father, Craig Langston, had given me his name and his artsyness, I didn't look anything like him. Actually, I had my great-grandmother's eyes, and her temperament too, at least that's what my dad said when he was mad at me.

I nodded to Matt. I was ready to go. I hoped I didn't puke in his truck. He'd probably dump me off on the side of the road. Sometimes, I secretly wondered to myself the same question my mother, my sister, and pretty much everybody had been asking me since I hooked up with him. Why?

I knew he was an ass. A few hours before, or was it minutes?, I couldn't be sure, I saw him come out of one of the upstairs bedrooms with Monica Gray, buttoning his shirt as he went down the stairs. Not that I really cared. Three months earlier I would have told him off for even considering asking me out. I searched the room for my black jean jacket I thought I remembered bringing. Man, that place was trashed! Some idiots were taking turns throwing their Styrofoam cups with beer still in them into the beautiful black marble fireplace.

I followed Matt down the tiled hallway and out the door to the crappy truck that he drove. It must have just started raining. I decided that after that night, I would break up with Matt. He really was kind of a loser.

Matt had trouble finding his truck. I noticed him swaying and asked, "Are you okay to drive?"

"Yeah, I'm fine. I didn't drink too much."

I rolled my eyes and got in the passenger seat. The old black Chevy had seen better days, and my seatbelt wouldn't fasten. After I tried a couple of times, Matt laughed and said, "Don't worry," his words slurred together, "I'm a good driver."

For just a split second, I thought I didn't care what happened. Maybe it would be better: a quick end to a wasted life.

Matt's crappy truck took a while to start, and then we pulled out on the highway toward home. Pandora started in the middle of an old song.

"I told you I hated that damn song!" Matt let go of the wheel for a second while he tried to reach his CD case that was lying on the floor. My heart lodged in my throat and the last thing I saw was a blinding light, and then, only darkness.

Chapter 2

EMILY

I tossed my cell phone onto the coffee table and flopped back on the couch to watch *Grey's Anatomy*. I had talked to Spencer for three hours, and my phone had gone dead. I smiled when I thought of him. He was blond and beautiful and awesome on the football field. We had been seeing a lot of each other these past six months. All my friends were jealous. Of course they were! He was the cutest guy on the football team, if not the school. He was a senior, a couple of years older than me, but I liked that. I got to go to everything with him, and when the prom came around, I got to go with him too.

We went out last night, and were supposed to go to the movies, but we ended up at his house. His parents were gone to some fundraiser so we were alone. Things got pretty heated and we almost did it. I wanted to, but he stopped us. He said he wanted to wait, and that he respected me. Wasn't that sweet? It just made me want him more. Mom loved him, unlike that douche bag Matt that Sam had been dating. Sure he was cute, but he was bad news. I thought Sam was just dating him to piss off Mom. Everyone was so worried about her, but I wasn't. I thought she just acted like that because she hated the fact that I was the center of attention for once.

It used to be so sickening. She made straight A's, Honor Society, band, the whole bit. I was practically invisible at our house. When she snuck out again tonight, I didn't tell Mom, not because I was protecting Sam, but mostly because I just didn't care what she did.

Something else about her that pissed me off was how unfair it was how she had always been Dad's favorite. Not that I cared that much, but still. He was my dad, too. Just because she got the "artsy" gene and wrote her stupid songs and poetry and played piano didn't mean she was better than me. She was such a nerd. She had been turning away from Dad and treating him like shit, too. I secretly loved this. Dad actually asked me out for breakfast, even though all he really wanted to do was ask me if I knew what was going on with Sam. What a joke.

Why did everyone think it was some big tragedy? I didn't. I thought she'd just finally showed her true black colors. She'd really been a pain in the ass in the past few months, and I could hardly stand her. Plus, I was really busy. Since I'd made the cheerleader squad I'd become popular. It was nice that it'd finally happened. I deserved it.

The home phone rang. Nobody ever called on that phone. I picked up.

"Emily." Mom was sobbing. Something about her voice sent a chill down my spine. "Sam's here," she said, "at the hospital. There's been a bad car wreck. Can you call your dad, and Nana?"

My heart felt like it stopped for a moment. I barely managed a "Yes, don't worry," and I hung up. If Sam's in Mom's unit, things were bad. My hand shook as I called Dad.

SAMANTHA

I stood barefoot in a field of endless amber wheat. When the breeze blew, the field rippled like the sea. The sky was a cloudless, perfect indigo. As I was strolled to an unknown destination, my hair blew loosely around my face.

In the distance, I saw a crystal clear pond. It appeared cool and inviting. When I got closer, I saw the water painted a sapphire blue, and the surface sparkled like a sea of jewels. The sun reflecting off the pond was not harsh like I had imagined, but a soft white light. Suddenly, I felt hot.

The sweat dripped down my neck between my breasts. My clothes felt too heavy on my body. I felt desperate to have the coolness of the water on my skin. I stepped out of my billowy black skirt and tugged the white peasant blouse I wore over my head. I dipped my toes into the water and sighed. It was just as refreshing as it seemed, and I began to wade in, then to swim.

I floated effortlessly on my back, not worried about anything. Suddenly, I felt a tugging toward the bottom of the pond. My waist, then my breasts, then my neck, and finally my head are underwater. I was still not afraid. The lure of the water was too appealing. I opened my eyes and looked downward. Instead of the light being above the water, it had moved under the water, and I found myself drawn to it. And, surprised, I realized I was able to breathe the water. The same to my lungs as air. I was a mermaid.

Without warning, the friendly water turned menacing in my lungs. I couldn't breathe. The water heaved out of my mouth, and when I tried to take another breath, the water assaulted my lungs. I began to panic. The liquid filled my lungs, my body, and my mind.

I woke up in an unfamiliar bed to a searing, unrelenting pain. My head felt disconnected from my body. Everything blurred, but I could make out the image of Mom's face. She spoke to me, but I couldn't answer. A tube lodged inside my throat. It felt too large, as if it actually expanded in my throat. I tried to reach up and take it out myself, but I couldn't because my hands were tied to the bed. People yelled at me in angry voices. Why were they mad? Why couldn't I get up? Why wouldn't my legs work? Suddenly, the darkness returned. The sweet, blissful darkness.

EDEN

Because I was nurse at the ICU, they let me get away with staying in Sam's room for longer than other patient's family members. Emily had gone home hours ago. There was really no use for her to stay because she couldn't be in the ICU for long. I spent most of the night in Sam's room, just sitting next to her and holding her hand. Matt, her boyfriend, had been killed in the crash. I heard the nurses whispering about it, because of confidentiality, but of course I would find out.

A few hours earlier, I watched as a couple of men with a stretcher went into the room next to Sam's and left shortly after. The family members that grieved out in the hallway saw them leave, but had no idea that their loved one rested on that stretcher because of its design. The hospital ordered that special kind of stretcher in bulk because it could hold a body in a cavity within its core. It was only used when transporting the dead. When the attendants left the room, the stretcher appeared empty, but it was not. The attendants traveled through the hospital without freaking other people out. They joked around, even rode on an elevator inches away from other people, and nobody knew the secret. The dead among the living, and no one was the wiser.

How well I knew that feeling.

I felt shock and sadness for the boy's parents. Sure, I didn't like him, but I could feel their pain, and just the gratefulness that Sam had made it. She shouldn't have. And she could still die. I braced myself for the truth: she probably *would* die. I knew it. I felt it. Those kinds of injuries, even if the patient survived, are rarely easy to recover from. Months of rehab were usually needed to help them walk, talk, even use a fork like they did before the accident.

As quickly as the nurse in me appeared, she became eclipsed by the mother in me. Memories of my pregnancy, how happy I was when I found out I was pregnant with Sam, flooded my mind. And Craig, so excited about being a dad and so sure she would be a girl, had painted the spare bedroom pink in a single day and created a beautiful moral on the wall by the crib. When she was born, Craig held her and, refusing to put her in the crib where she would be alone, held her for 24 hours straight. It was only until he fell asleep that I was able to take her from his arms.

When I last saw my Sam, she had been confused and combative. She remained on a ventilator. Dr. Combs, the neurologist, had been in to talk to me. They would be doing the surgery in about an hour. There were special considerations because Sam was pregnant. Pregnant! Even so, it had been made plain to me that there was a very good chance Sam would miscarry. In my heart, I didn't care. I didn't want to exchange my baby for a baby I didn't know. Maybe she would miscarry and the pregnancy wouldn't be an issue. How could I think such a thing?

Sam was pregnant. I couldn't get my mind around that. I hadn't told anyone yet. Nana hadn't made it to the hospital yet, and I hadn't seen Craig. What a surprise. I knew he had to travel from Austin, but he acted like I exaggerated. He never believed things are as bad as they are, like I had somehow made it up from thin air. Emily called him, and told him to call me, and I tried to explain what had happened. Our daughter had been in a terrible car accident. She has a head bleed. She might be paralyzed. I didn't tell him about the pregnancy. I couldn't make myself form the words.

I guessed it was probably Matt's baby. Of course. She'd never really spent too much time with any of the other boys. I mean, I knew she'd been dating around, but she never saw any of them more than once. As far as I knew, which wasn't much. I didn't even really know where they had sex. Well, I knew that Sam had been struggling, and had not been herself, but I refused to believe she was sleeping around with different guys. She hadn't changed that much in those last few months.

A baby! My eyes teared up for the millionth time. What were we going to do? My hopes of getting Sam back on the track to Julliard were crushed. She would have to give the baby up. Of course. There was no other solution. She would not get an abortion, I knew that much. At least I thought I knew. I always thought I was anti-abortion, until then.

The surgery techs in their blue caps and scrubs came to get Sam, along with a respiratory therapist to control the ventilator. I kissed her bruised cheek and got ready to wait.

Just then, I heard a familiar voice asking about Sam. I knew that voice anywhere. Craig had arrived. He saw me standing outside Sam's room. Even then, when I was angry, I still felt that old attraction to him. He had a lean build, like an artist should, dark hair that had the "on purpose" messy look. I knew he probably spent an hour getting it that way. I noticed small touches of gray here and there, and a few wrinkles I hadn't seen before. His eyes, lovely, perfect, the color of coffee, still got to me.

He wore a pink button-up shirt, with the top two buttons undone, gray tie with pink and white swirls, gray slacks, and Italian leather shoes. He always did have an almost girl-like obsession with clothes and shoes. Even now, he took my breath away. There I stood, in my scrubs from the night before, no shower or anything. Seeing Craig always made me feel self-conscious, like I somehow never measured up. *Why should I care what I'm wearing? For God's sake, I'd been there for over 24 hours.*

"Eden." He nodded to me, as if we are professional acquaintances. As if we'd never made love, or had children together. "She's in there, right?" he asked, getting ready to enter.

"Actually, no," I said quietly. "They just took her to surgery."

"Oh," Craig said, as he ran his manicured fingers through his dark hair. "Well, that's good, right, because they think there is something they can fix surgically?"

"Well, possibly." I tried to explain. "Sam has a head bleed. There is blood in her brain. They are going to try to relieve the pressure. If they can't . . ."

"How typical," he muttered, sounding frustrated. "Miss Gloom and Doom. Try to look at the bright side, for once!" He raised his voice.

"Something else I need to tell you."

He stared at me warily.

"Sam's pregnant."

Chapter 3

ELIZABETH

When I finally got to the hospital, it was late. I had my handicap tags so I could park wherever I wanted, and I took advantage of that. I might have been old, but I could still drive and get around okay.

It hadn't been too terribly long since I was in the hospital myself. I was puttering around in my flowerbeds about six months earlier when I started feeling sick. I was sweating and having trouble breathing. I went into the house and managed to call 911 before I passed out. When I woke up, a couple of paramedics were putting oxygen on my face and trying to get me to talk to them.

I really hate hospitals, pretty much everything about them: fighting for a place to park, the perky volunteers in their ugly yellow smocks the color of old mustard, the antiseptic smell mixing with the scent of floor wax. I hated the feeling of panic I got whenever I visited one. It's been a rare day that I went to the hospital for a good reason. I know it's unreasonable, but there it was.

I asked at the desk about the location of the ICU, and made my way slowly down the hall. I wanted to move faster, but my arthritis hindered me. A couple of nuns, one young, one old, seemed to float past me. They met my eyes for a second, and I saw real kindness there, not fabricated.

Something about the religious feel of the hospital did comfort me, though. It reminded me of my husband, who passed away some time ago. I could almost feel his arms around me then, his comforting whisper in my ear.

When I got to the ICU, I saw Craig, Eden's ex-husband, standing next to her in front of Bed Four. They were having a hushed, but angry discussion. Boy had I seen that before. I went over to her and gave her a hug.

"Eden, where is Sam?" I got right to the point.

"She's in surgery," Eden explained, her eyes red from crying.

Craig started pacing nervously back and forth.

"Nana, I need to talk to you," Eden said.

The three of us left the unit and made our way to the waiting room. That time of night it's empty. We found a couple of seats, the kind made for skinny people with no thighs that apparently only stay in one position. I sat down next to her. Her hands were trembling. I took her young, smooth hand in mine. In comparison, my hand was covered with age spots and my fingers were bent with arthritis. "What is it, child?" I asked her, feeling like I was about to fall off a cliff.

My breath caught in my throat. How I loved her. She had lost some weight since I'd seen her, probably from worrying about Sam.

"You know that Samantha was in a bad car accident." She paused for a moment, and I nodded to encourage her to finish. "The truck they were in flipped twice and the driver, Sam's boyfriend, was killed in the crash." I sucked in a breath of air. "Sam is not in good shape. Her right arm and right leg are broken, her eyes are swollen, but otherwise her face is okay. She is being operated on by the neurosurgeon as we speak. They are trying to relieve some of the pressure in her skull. In addition, she has a minor bleed. They are using exploratory surgery to determine if they can help it. It could go either way."

I saw her eyes tearing through the blur of my own vision. My heart threatened to beat out of its chest.

"All of this is complicated by the fact that . . ." She took another deep breath, and I wasn't sure if she was going to finish. I simply waited for her to compose herself. Finally, her green eyes met mine. "Nana, Sam is pregnant."

"What?" I demanded. I felt myself falling, falling off the ledge. "How can this be? Was that boy the father?" A million questions came to mind, swirling around until they didn't make any sense.

"We don't know. I guess. We can't ask her, either. She is totally out of it, and on a ventilator."

For the first time since I got there, I saw Eden. I mean, really saw her. Her hair, the color of red autumn leaves, was once in a messy bun, had fallen out and begun to escape down her shoulders. Her makeup, or what was left of it, smudged. Under her eyes, there were black circles. Her scrubs, which she always presses, were wrinkled and dirty.

Craig was useless as usual. He spoke up. "I have told Eden repeatedly to not be so negative, but she just can't seem to handle it. Being so pessimistic is not going to help Sam get better."

Eden slammed her fist down on the coffee table. "Damn it, Craig! Thinking about rainbows and unicorns is not going to help either."

The three of us sat there in silence, hearing only the sound of our own hearts beating.

EDEN

I was glad Nana was here. She had always been my rock. She'd raised me since I was fifteen, since Mama died. I still thought about my mother every day. In many ways, Sam looked just like her. Except for the hair color she had every one of my mother's features. A splash of freckles across the bridge of her nose, the same dimple in her left cheek. Even the birthmark on her leg reminded me of the one my mother had. Most of all, she had the same eyes. Eyes that were so expressive, sometimes they were too intense to look at directly, like trying to stare at the sun.

Some of the mannerisms were the same as well. The way she twirled her hair around her finger when she read or watched T.V. The same intense expression when she was caught up in playing the piano, or painting in oils, or taking pictures with her camera. I just hoped Sam, if she made it, didn't die young, like Mama.

Being there in the hospital as a family member was altogether different. When working my shift, each patient, while they may be an individual, was a job I needed to finish. After I had finished giving medications and doing assessments and giving report to the day-shift nurse, I could go home. There was a comfort in that. Don't get me wrong. I loved being a nurse. I didn't mind the long hours or working on the holidays or getting puked or peed or bled on. I felt like I was helping people. Maybe in some small way, I could make up for the wrong I'd done. Maybe, I could get my karma back on track. Maybe, the wrongs I had done in my past had resulted in what had transpired with Sam.

I felt the old panic rising in my throat. My hands trembled, my throat closed off, and I couldn't breathe. My face flushed with heat while my heart thudded in my chest.

Even as an insider, so to speak, there were things I couldn't do. I couldn't examine Sam's chart, or find Sam's X-rays or CT scans in the computer, even though I did those things every day for strangers. Not for my child. Not for my baby that I'd carried in my womb for nine months and fed from my breast. Nana wanted to send me home for rest, but I couldn't. Not until the neurosurgeon came back. I had to be there, to find out what happened, how everything progressed or declined, what her chances were. If she made it at all. And if the baby, oh God, my grandchild, was going to make it.

I sat in the darkened waiting room with a Coke and a package of Fritos, my thoughts going to Sam. And not just the current terror, but the change I had seen in her this year. Not only had she started to resemble Mama physically but in her personality as well. I couldn't understand it. It was like seeing Mama all over again. I tried so hard with Sam to give her the best life ever, and to be the best mother. God knows I had screwed up, but didn't effort count at all? I wanted so much for her to have the perfect life, the white house and picket fence. I couldn't help thinking, though, the old adage of 'What goes around comes around.' Maybe I was finally getting paid back for what I'd done all those years ago. My family was being torn apart, much the way I destroyed someone else's family. I never thought I would be sitting in the same room I sat in all those years ago, waiting to find out if Sam was okay, just like I sat here waiting for word on Mama.

December 1985

Sarah and I got off the bus at the stop by my house. All in all it had been a good day. For one thing, I didn't have to go to school until the New Year. Sarah and I strolled the rest of the way home together, giggling and talking about what a pain Mrs. Quinn was and how we wished we didn't have to have her for English next semester. Sarah was my next-door neighbor. She was a good choice for a best friend. Kind and funny, she usually didn't ask too many questions about my life with Mama. I thought it was because she thought she wouldn't like the answers. But that was okay as long as I didn't have to reveal too much of myself to her. When I was with Sarah, I could talk about teenage things, like bands I liked and what movie was coming out. Sarah was always up for a good movie.

She was also pretty much my opposite in the looks department. Her hair was shorter and dark, yet in a cool haircut. Her parents had a bit more money, since nobody was an alcoholic at their house, and so she was usually dressed to the nines. I wore the same five T-shirts over again, and whatever I could steal from Mama when she was out of it, along with my stonewashed jeans and Converse shoes. My red hair had gotten so long, and since Mama wouldn't ever sober up enough to take me to get a haircut, I just wadded the whole thing up in a ponytail and called it good.

I turned my key in the lock and, still smiling at Sarah, who waved as she left, and let myself in. I hoped that Mom was up already. Usually she was sleeping. She slept a lot the past few months since her boyfriend, Randy, had been coming over so much. Sometimes they stayed up till four or five in the morning, drinking, arguing, making up, and having sex. My room was right across from them and I could hear everything. Too many nights I stared at the ceiling with my pillow pressed around my ears so I didn't hear them. It never worked. Mama never had to give me the birds and the bees talk. I heard it all the time, and more than once had seen my mom and her latest in various stages of dress.

I didn't really know what Mama saw in Randy. Mama was so beautiful. Her hair was a beautiful golden blond. Her legs were lean and went on forever. Even her name, Diane, sounded sexy. A lot of the men in Tulsa, where we lived, wanted Mama. I hoped I would look just like her when I grew up. I was on my way for sure. Boys were starting to notice me already, even though I was only fifteen. I seemed more like seventeen, or even eighteen if I had makeup on. I had my first period when I was only nine, and the boobs came soon after. I always felt awkward about that. Being the tallest girl from the sixth grade on didn't put me in any popularity contests.

But back to Randy. I really didn't like Randy. Randy was the epitome of the term "loser." Long brown hair, shower optional, the ever-present stoner was the latest in jerks Mama brought home. There was always a combination of pot and body odor emanating from his armpits. And sometimes, I would catch him staring at me in a creepy way.

The best I could hope for was that Mama would get tired of him and move on. I started to get worried, though, because he seemed to be lasting longer than the others. Instead of learning their names, I kept track of them by their occupations, since I always wished that Mama would accidentally find a good one that was up for the job of daddy. Frank "Greasy Mechanic" lasted two weeks. Then Julian, A.K.A. "The Accountant", lasted only a few days. Next came Brad, who I liked to refer to as the "One-Hit-Wonder". He'd lasted only one day. But Randy, so far, had held on to Mama for six months now. He stayed over almost every night at first. He only went home because he didn't have clothes over at our house, or else he needed to score some drugs.

Mama and Randy had a huge fight a couple of nights ago, and I hoped it was over, except I knew it wasn't. At least for Mama. She cried all the time and made me worry. I saw more needles lying around the house, and I knew she was doing more heroin. She was barely sober or awake at all. It was awfully hard to be around Mama when she was depressed like that.

The fact that Randy had not been around for a few days was making Mama crazy. This happened once before. When he didn't come over or call for a few days, Mama went through her routine. First, she would sit by the phone for a few hours. Mama always made such a fool of herself for him. Then she would pretend she didn't care and suddenly she wanted to spend lots of time with me. That never lasted, but how I longed for it. I bloomed under her love and attention, and always wanted more. It was never enough for me, and I thought at times my neediness was too much for her. When too much time had gone by and Randy hadn't come over, she would call him, pretending like she just wanted to chat. Randy usually couldn't resist her when she would do that, but it seemed that he had started to get tired of her. She had to call more, and make a bigger fuss, to get a response out of him. That was unprecedented. Tonight he didn't even answering his phone. Mama was furious. She slammed the phone down on its receiver.

The next thing I knew, she called Julian, the accountant. Ah, Stage Two. When Mama failed to achieve the response she needed, she called one of her previous guys, and got his hopes up that he had a chance. Then she would have him take her somewhere where she knew the guy she was mad at would see them together. In this case, she got Julian to take her to the club where Randy played guitar.

"What, Sweetie?" I heard her purring on the phone when I came into the kitchen.

"I've been thinking about you. I miss you, don't you miss me?"

I heard that sound in her voice, the sound her voice had when she came out of the bedroom partially dressed after a long night with Randy.

Sometimes, I stood in front of the mirror, pretending to be Mama. I practiced pouting my lips, and giving flirty expressions. I practiced walking the way she did. I practiced tipping my head the way she did when she thought you were 'trying to pull a fast one on her', as she put it. I practiced putting my hands on my hips and moving them seductively.

I threw my books onto the table and opened the fridge. There was nothing to eat except cheese, a few slices of stale bread, and one can of soda. Mom wasn't too good at shopping either, and she didn't need to eat much. Most of the time she simply forgot to eat. She was on a liquid diet; liquid whiskey, liquid vodka, liquid whatever she could find. I often tried to forget to eat like Mama, but my stomach would not be silenced. Sometimes I went to Sarah's house, hoping they would be having dinner. I saw the pity in their eyes, and I had to look away. Sarah's mom did not like Mama. Most mothers didn't. It was because of the natural way she had with men, making them do things without them even realizing it.

Mama's plan must have worked. Suddenly, she was singing and humming to herself. She got dressed in a green, low-cut dress that accented her creamy skin, brushed her golden hair until it shone, and put on her makeup. She saw me watching her in the mirror.

"Remember, Eden," she said, as she put on her mascara, "don't put on your makeup all thick like pancake batter like ugly women do. You and me, we're already pretty. We don't need that. The best way to use makeup is to make it seem like you don't need no help. See how my skin is soft? See how perfect it is?"

Sometimes, I cringed when Mama would speak. She was beautiful, but especially when she was excited, you could hear the hill-talk dialect come through. She'd run away from the cabin on the river the minute she could, and never looked back. She had the body of Marilyn Monroe, but she talked like Ellie Mae from *The Beverly Hillbillies*. I've worked my whole life to not pick up her horrible accent.

"I'll bet some people would think I was your older sister, not your momma. Do you think?" She waited for my approval. She knew I'd agree. I was in awe of Mama. Everybody was. You couldn't help it.

Julian came over to pick up Mama. If I could have picked one guy to see Mama with, it would be him. He had a steady job, and from the looks of his clothes and car (he drove a Mercedes) he had loads of cash. He was tall and lean and probably spent more money on hair care products in a week than I did in a year. He glanced at his expensive watch as he waited impatiently for Mama.

I couldn't believe he would date someone like Mama. I mean, Mama was gorgeous and all, but Julian was out of her league. Plus, I couldn't see him wanting to be a husband to Mama. Men didn't see her as wife material. They treated her like trash because, well, she was. I knew in my heart nobody would ever want Mama for a wife, or me for a kid.

I never knew my real dad. Mama would never talk about it, except to say things like, "That was a long time ago, Eden Rain."

Yeah, my name's Eden. I'm pretty sure Mama was high when she named me. Most the time I didn't mind my name. It set me apart from the rest of the airheads at my school. I didn't have any friends except for Sarah, and that was okay with me. Those silly girls weren't people I wanted to hang around with anyway. Still, I wished for a dad that would show up when I received first place in the science fair, or when I got the Outstanding Math Student award.

Years later, I finally got the story out of Nana. Apparently, my dad didn't even know I existed. She went to a Creedence Clearwater Revival Concert with some girlfriends, and they hooked up with some stoner guys they met there. Mama had had a one-night stand with this guy named Jeff, probably in the back of his van or something great like that. Long story short, she barely knew his name, and certainly not what he did for a living or where he lived or anything. Apparently, there was not a lot of heart-to-heart soul-searching dialogue between the two of them. I was the product of that meeting. Free love and all that jazz. How lovely.

I knew that Mama loved me, somewhere deep down inside, but most the time I couldn't tell. I thought she just kept me around because she never was sober enough to figure out how to get rid of me. I heard a story once about how she took me to a party and forgot me there for two days before she came back. Her stoner friends fed me god knows what until they were able to reach her. They would have called the cops before that but didn't want the cops coming over to their house and looking around too closely.

Mama never understood my passion for school. "I didn't graduate sixth grade and look how I turned out!" she would say, a cigarette between her fingers and a *True Confessions* magazine in her other hand while she sunbathed in the yard. *Yeah, look how you tuned out, Mama. Awesome.*

So I worked really hard in school. I loved science and math and biology, and I always thought I would like to go to med school one day. But, if you hadn't noticed, most doctors came from families with money. Mama would see my textbooks lying around the house, and she'd do inconsiderate things like leave an ashtray on top of my novel I was reading for English lit. Classy.

It's really surprising that I turned out as well as I did. I doubt Mama quit drinking or smoking when she was pregnant with me. At least she didn't do heroin or LSD then. Isn't that a horrible thing to have to say? At least she didn't do heroin or LSD, like that's some kind of twisted consolation prize.

After Julian left, I made myself a cheese sandwich and watched television for a while. Most nights I spent alone like that, unless I went to Sarah's house. I loved it over there. Her mom made dishes like pot roast and mashed potatoes or spaghetti and meatballs and they almost always had dessert. Once, when I mentioned to Mama how I wished we would have dinners like that she snorted, "Really? Well, no, thank you. Do you wish you were fat like your little friend Sarah? Or that I looked like her mother, a chubby June Cleaver? I think I'll pass." Then she took a few more diet pills so she wouldn't be hungry.

I had tears in my eyes from those remarks. Yes, Sarah's mom was a little overweight, at least by Mama's standards, which was anyone over a size 4, but she was so nice and loved Sarah so much. Sarah wasn't fat either. I would still have traded Mama for Joy though. She actually *cared* about things like homework and report cards, and going to school on Open House night when their daughters had projects on display. Mama never went to those things. It used to bother me a lot, but when I finally convinced her to go, I was sorry. She spent the whole time flirting with Sarah's dad and half a dozen other men. I felt so ashamed.

The other thing I liked about going to Sarah's house was talking to her dad. Bruce was really nice, and helped me with my geometry when I got stuck. He was pleasant and easy to talk to. I had to admit I had a little crush on him. He wasn't extremely great looking, but he had a nice haircut and pretty brown eyes the color of chocolate, very straight teeth, and was muscular from working out. And the thing was, he was a really good dad to Sarah and her little brother, Cody. He went to all their school plays and PTA meetings, and did things like helping Cody build a kite from scratch and teaching Sarah how to drive, even though she wasn't supposed to. So you can see why I liked going over there so much. It kind of did seem a lot like the Cleavers. And I also had to admit that I never really thought of him as a man until that day at school when Mama was flirting with him.

ELIZABETH

I finally talked Eden into going home for a few hours. I knew she hadn't eaten a bite, probably since Sam had been admitted. Eden was an intense person to begin with, very analytical, very left-brained. Also, she was a worrier beyond reason. She had always been that way. Well, as far as I knew.

I leaned over and whispered to Samantha, "Hey, Sweetie, it's Nana." There was no sound in the room except for the *whoosh* of the ventilator and the beeps of the monitor.

I held her hand and we were both quiet for a while, then I said, "Samantha, I can see that you are struggling. Struggling is life. We all do it. The main thing is, women in our family have made it through some tough times, and this is no different." I studied her bruised face, covered with bandages, and her body, practically in a cast from head to toe.

"I've been meaning to see you, to spend some more time with you, but I haven't been able to," I said, gently brushing away a lock of her auburn hair that had fallen across her forehead. "Enough is enough, Samantha Kaye. You have to come back to us. There's so much I wanted to tell you before I went home. Remember how you used to love my stories when you were little? I used to tell you stories about unicorns and fairies, knights-in-shining-armor and damsels-in-distress, of Indian princesses and talking animals. Now I think it's time you heard some different kinds of stories." I stroked her hand and fought the urge to sob.

"I know you are hiding some secret from me. I know about secrets, you know. I have a few myself." I watched the rise and fall of Samantha's chest, and imagined the beating of her heart. I heard the nurses out in the hallway talking to each other. I heard the sounds of the lunch trays being passed out.

"So here's the deal, as you always put it. I'm going to come here every day and sit with you. I'll tell you all my secrets. Then, maybe, you can tell me yours and we can move on through this horrible time in our lives, okay? I'll tell you stories about the women in this family and what we have had to endure, what we have made it through. You can draw strength through me, strength to make you better. I'll just sit here for a piece and tell you my story first, okay? You don't mind, do you, child?" I asked, kissing her cheek.

I decided to come to the hospital every day until Sam was released and tell her about her family. I would record it as well with a mini-tape recorder as I talked, then find somebody to dictate it to when it was finished. I felt that if

Sam could hear me, as people always said that coma patients could, maybe my story and the stories of her grandmother and mother would give her the strength to come through this. Maybe. What did I have to lose but everything?

The next morning I came back to the hospital, prepared to stay a while. I brought my medication with me, my knitting, an extra pillow, and a few snacks. I settled down in the recliner next to Sam's bed and reached over to kiss her forehead.

"Hello, Sweet Pea," I said, fussing with her blankets. "It's Nana. I'm here to tell you stories today, remember?" I smoothed her hair back and tried not to see the paleness of her skin. I tried to tune out the beeping of the monitors and the nurses' chitchat in the halls. "Let's see, where to begin. I'm not sure. Now here's the thing, my Sammie. A lot of what I'm going to tell you is not pretty. But neither is life. It's wonderful and terrible and heart-wrenching all at the same time."

Something had been bringing back the ghosts from the past. The last time I'd felt this way was when my sister was born. It was a funny thing about being old. I couldn't remember what happened yesterday, but I vividly remembered that morning in 1940, when I was seventeen.

I had overslept. I wasn't sure exactly what had happened and why I hadn't been able to wake up. I jumped up from the pallet of blankets on the floor. The cabin had more of a chill than normal. Daddy would be upset if he knew I hadn't got the fire started and at least coffee made.

Usually, I had to get up early to get a jump on the chores. The fact that I had slept in had already put me way behind. Mama wasn't up cooking breakfast as usual. Was this one more chore I would be expected to take on? How much more could I take? It had been difficult at best, because I had been juggling homework, the chores, and caring for Jacob, my younger brother. I also had an older brother named Billy, but he was gone already, probably trying to find some work. Mama was usually up by now.

"Mama?" I slowly pushed open the tattered curtain that separated her and Daddy's room from the main living area. Mama was still in bed. I tiptoed over to check on her, and she turned over with a moan. Then I saw the crimson blood pooled around her, soaking her sheets, dripping onto the floor. It seemed like she was bathing in it. I did not scream. I was used to the feeling of fear. So familiar, in fact, that fear, instead of an emotion, had become an unwelcome lover, his icy fingers forever stroking me.

The day my sister was born was not a day I would ever forget. Mama's labor took all of the morning, and continued into the early morning hours of the next day. I shuddered at the memory; the eerie glow of the roaring fireplace, the crackle of the embers meshing with Mama's screams, the old cook stove smoking up the house, and me, trying to keep up with the mountains of towels that were being washed and used and washed again. The midwife's worried face, then her badly concealed fear.

Mama kept crying out Daddy's name, but Daddy wasn't there. Mama's sweaty brow furrowed over her blank eyes. Something was wrong. The baby wasn't coming, and nobody knew how to find the doc.

If only Daddy was here, I remembered thinking. *Mama needs Daddy to be here.*

I remember running down the uneven terrain of our land. Not pausing to put on my boots, my bare feet felt numb from the cold. Tree branches scratched my face as I covered more land, the soles of my feet impervious to rocks, exposed tree roots, even holes.

I had a feeling I knew right where Daddy was. Some of the gossip around town had found its way to my ear, and I had even been in a scuffle at school about it. I hoped against hope it wasn't true, but something inside me knew it was.

I came to a dead stop, my chest heaving, and sweat rolling down my face. I stood in front of a pretty white house on the nice side of town. I opened the matching white picket gate and closed it. Beautiful rose bushes of different colors climbed up the side of the house. The trim was a cheerful yellow, matching the daisies growing in the flowerbox mounted outside the crystal clean windows.

I raised my fist to knock, but almost lost my courage more than once. How long I stood there, I'm not sure. I eyed my tattered nightgown, a result of Mama mending and mending until it seemed the dress was no longer much fabric, but more like strings of thread than anything. My bare feet were dirty and bleeding. My hair, disheveled and undone from my ribbon, pasted flat to my face. I felt ashamed about my appearance.

Leaning forward, I used my knees for support as I tried to catch my breath. Finally, only because I remembered Mama's screams for Daddy, I found the courage to knock on the door. I heard a woman's laugh, and some undecipherable words that sounded like she was teasing somebody. The door opened and I stood face-to-face with the most beautiful woman I had ever seen. Her dark black hair fell softly down her shoulders. Between her manicured fingers she held a cigarette. Her soft white bathrobe strained with the weight of her ample breasts and clung to her hourglass shaped body. Her skin, a creamy white, had not a single wrinkle or freckle to mar its beauty. Her sultry blue eyes rested on my own. Bedroom eyes. I had never really understood that term until I saw that woman.

She took one last drag of her cigarette and said huskily, "Well, I don't know your name, but I know who you belong to. Jonas, one of your kids is here."

I heard my father's gruff voice curse in the background. Seconds later, he appeared, only half-dressed. I lowered my eyes. My cheeks burned with humiliation.

Daddy's huge frame filled the doorway. He, like always, drunk. Red lipstick covered his mouth and neck. He had a shadow of whiskers covering his chin. His red eyes looked blankly at me.

"I don't know what you're talkin' about, Darlin'." He yawned. "She ain't mine. I don't know who she is." He leaned over, his breath reeking of whiskey. He tried to shut the door, but I stepped in front of it.

"Daddy, it's Mama. The baby's not coming like it should and she's bad off." I choked back a sob. "You need to come home," I demanded. I could not believe how brave I felt.

"You get out of here, you hear? Go help your ma or somethin'. And don't come here again." He had to hold on to the doorway for support.

"Please, Daddy," I somehow found the courage to say. "She needs you awfully bad." I paused, then repeated, "The midwife is worried about them both."

At the mention of the baby, Pa leaned out the door and spat on the ground. "Serves her right. Told her I didn't want no more kids." He ran his fingers through his dark hair.

"Daddy, please, you have to come!" I started to plead again. Suddenly, a flash of pain and I was on the ground. My hand rose to my cheek, reddened from the blow.

"I told you to get out of here!" Daddy bellowed. "Leave me be!"

As I stumbled to stand up, I heard a child crying in the background of the woman's house. Hurriedly, she shut the door.

I went back home, my face stinging from Daddy's fist, tears streaming down my face. But more than the physical pain was the pain from his denial that I was his child, and the continuing rejection of the rest of us as well. *Damn you, Daddy*, I thought to myself.

When I got back to the cabin, I heard a chilling scream. I ran to the bedroom just in time to see the baby slip out of Mama in a bath of blood and fluids. Mama fell back onto the pillow, her face dripping, her hair soaked.

A few minutes later, Mama started screaming again. There was a flurry of activity, and the midwife handed me the baby. My heavy heart lightened for a moment when I held my baby sister.

"It's twins!" the midwife cried, and went to Mama's side to help the other baby out. I held the baby that she had given me, wrapped in a blanket but still covered with afterbirth. Mama cried out in a sound that I have never forgotten, and another baby emerged. The midwife took the baby and held it up. Not a peep issued from the tiny form.

"Stillborn," she confirmed.

I saw the baby. Blue and smaller than the one I held. It was a boy.

Mama cried like I had never heard anyone cry. "Let me hold him," she begged.

The midwife hesitated, but handed the tiny bundle over to Mama.

Mama kissed the baby and said, "I would have named you Jonas. Maybe, you would have made things better . . ." she said, trailing off.

"Mama," I said, with tears in my eyes, "you still have a baby girl," and I gave her my sister.

"What do you want to name her?" I asked.

Mama just shook her head weakly. She was pale, paler than the snow that fell in February. She couldn't hold her head up.

Finally, she whispered, "You can name her, Elizabeth. Please, take care of her for me."

"No, Mama," I sobbed. "Don't leave us, Mama."

But Mama died that night. Someone had found the doctor and told him to come, but it was too late. Mama had lost too much blood. I looked on, but didn't cry a tear, as the nurse bathed Mama and put her in her Sunday dress.

Some of our neighbors made Mama's coffin. A kind friend of Mama's, her best friend, Isabelle O'Neill, took care of Delilah. Isabelle's husband, David, his son, Henry, and some of the same neighbors that built the coffin came to dig the grave. Their questioning eyes rested on me. They wanted to know where Daddy was. I couldn't, wouldn't say.

The last time I saw Mama was when they put her in that plain pine box, and they put the baby in with her. When David nailed down the lid, I felt each nail in my heart. I felt each nail in my future.

The frozen mountain ground stubbornly refused to open. The rocky soil that made for poor gardens seemed impossibly full of rocks that day. Several attempts were made with the worn shovels before the land succumbed, yielding like a virgin to unwanted intercourse. I could not look away, thinking that the gaping hole they meant to put Mama in seemed too close to hell. I thought more than once that I wished that hole were for Daddy.

I sobbed bitterly, not just for Mama, but for Delilah, my brothers Jacob and Billy, and me. A wintry wind from the north blew in and chilled us all to the bone. It started sprinkling, then the heavens opened up and vomited an icy rain. Seemed fitting that it should rain on that horrible day.

Somehow, the news had made it back to Daddy. He showed up at the small rural cemetery looking like he hadn't slept, his hair a mess, his clothes wrinkled. His three-day beard gave him more the appearance of a handsome vagrant than of a man who had come to bury his wife. The preacher had to shout to make himself heard over the thunder.

The icy wind blew the rain into my eyes, and it stung. The rain mixed with my tears until I couldn't see. Preacher Jones made the service short, and everyone ran to take cover from the storm. I stood holding little Jacob's hand, with Billy at my side at the edge of Mama's grave. My worn dress, the same one I had worn yesterday when Delilah was born, soaked my skin.

I watched as the mountain dirt, with its shades of chocolate and red clay, mixed with the rain and turn into mud. I have never forgotten seeing it ooze its way onto the plain wooden coffin. I shuddered, thinking of Mama in her icy grave. It was truly the stuff of nightmares. I glanced across the grave at Daddy. He at least had the decency to appear to be grievin'. His eyes, raw with some unknown emotion and guilt, met mine, and he appeared taken aback by my glare. He left without saying anything.

I was seventeen years old the year I found out about Daddy's other woman, and the day my Mama died. That was the day the ember of hate started growing in my heart. I decided that from then on, I would be the one in control. No man, not Daddy, not anyone, was going to treat me or my sister like a dog.

It seemed unfair the way men always did what they wanted, seemingly with no consequence. I named my sister after the lady in the bible that ruined Sampson. She would be strong, too. That's what it was going to be like for us. I whispered that promise to her, and let her hold my pinkie. Her tiny hand gripped my finger tight, like she understood.

I really only knew Eden as a teenager. Her mother, my daughter, Diane, and I had a falling out and never spoke to each other after she left. I couldn't speak to her. When Diane turned eighteen, she left War Eagle and never came back. She said she couldn't wait to leave that hick town where nothing ever happened. We didn't even have a stoplight. Diane craved adventure. Oh, she also liked men, alcohol, and drugs. The Big Three. I remember once, when I had finally tracked her down, I called her to see how she was. She was my daughter, after all.

But Diane didn't want to talk to me. She never did. We were like oil and water, never destined to get along. I had some concerns about her drinking too much and probably doing some harder drugs than she admitted, but I had no proof. Diane made it clear I was not to interfere. I actually didn't know Eden existed until she was fifteen. That's how close Diane and I were. When Carolyn moved into town, she seemed rich by our hill folk standards, but now I realize it wasn't that she was so very rich, it just seemed that way because we were so very poor. Carolyn was a prostitute, or she had been, until she met Daddy. She fell head over heels for him. Before Daddy was such a drunk, most women would not be able to take their eyes off of him. He was, as Mama used to say, "A looker." When he did work, he did hard manual labor, so he was always lean and strong. Even though Irish-Scottish blood ran through his veins, the Cherokee Indian in him dominated his looks. He had the high cheekbones, the dark hair, and skin of a Cherokee, but the green eyes of an Irishman. Put together, these two traits proved irresistible to women.

When Daddy got married, most of the women in the town stopped pursuing him. Most of them knew Mama and loved her. It was hard not to. She was kind and helpful, and always the first one to respond if any of the hill folk were ailing or dying. Even if we did not have much, we could always spare a pan of cornbread or a lemon buttermilk pie.

There were always a few women who did not care that Daddy was married. For example, Rita Logan, who lived on the other side of the river, never gave up on Daddy. He was never really interested in her, though. But when Carolyn moved into town, something in Daddy changed. He disappeared more often, sometimes for days at a time. Mama knew something was up. It wasn't the first time Daddy had another woman, but it was the first time that he had a woman he seemed to care about.

Daddy's unhappiness and restlessness spilled over into our home. He begun to compare Mama to Carolyn, first, in subtle ways, without words, like the time he held up Mama's dress from the laundry and looked at it with such repulsion it made me cry. Yes, Mama had gained weight. Yes, Mama had gotten a little gray around the edges. I had never thought about how a man would look at Mama, or at me.

One night, Daddy quit beating around the bush and just said what he felt. I was busy shelling peas at the table next to Mama when Daddy started a fight.

"Why don't ya fix your hair sometimes?" he asked her, and not for the first time. It was always a comment like that. "Why don't ya ever make yourself any pretty clothes anymore," or "You know, you don't really need that second piece of corn bread. God, woman. If I want a pig, I'll bring one in from the yard." It was always after he had a few shots of whiskey.

Mama pretended not to hear and continued peeling potatoes for dinner. Sometimes, Daddy just talked to hear himself. Mama would usually ignore him when he was like that, but sometimes he would demand she answer him. And sometimes, if she didn't answer right away, he'd start swinging. That day, that horrible day that is etched in my memory, was one of those days.

Angry at being ignored, he took the bowl out of her hands, and threw it to the floor. The potatoes fell, the cold glass of the bowl splintered across the floor. I sat still in my chair, petrified, unable to speak or breathe.

"Why should I fix my hair?" she yelled back. "Will that make you stay here with me? Will that keep you away from her?" She sobbed.

"Woman, you disgust me," Daddy said. "You used to be so fine, with your pretty brown hair all tied in ribbons, and wearing that yella dress your mama made you. You had a figure, a waistline. What happened to ya?" he asked, staring at Mama as if she were nothing, like she was the dirt on his boots. "Answer me!" he roared.

I covered my ears.

Mama rose in a fury. "I'll tell you what happened!" she fumed, her fair skin reddened in anger. "Being married to you is what happened! Havin' your kids is what happened!" She sat down, anger gone, tears still streamed down her face. "Bein' stuck with you in this shack, never havin' nothin', never seein' nobody, and you, never wantin' me anymore!" It seemed now like a dam had broken loose, and all of Mama's unhappiness was spilling forth, flooding the entire world.

Stop Mama, I wanted to say, but couldn't. I knew she was going too far. But she continued. "Losin' two babies is what happened! Tryin' to make sure the kids have food to eat and clothes on their backs, and keeping up with the chores while you go whorin'! That's what happened! Being your *wife* is what happened!"

At that, Daddy made a fist and knocked Mama out of her chair. I jumped up and pressed myself into a corner, wanting to help Mama but unable to. At least, I thought to myself, Billy had taken Jacob berry picking, and they weren't going to be back for a while.

Mama cried softly, shielding her face from the blow. He began to hit her, over and over, until finally I couldn't take it anymore.

"Daddy, *stop it*!" I yelled, pummeling him with my fists that might as well have been made out of pillows for all the good they did. He stopped hitting Mama for a minute and knocked me to the floor. I cringed when Mama screamed. "Elizabeth, get out of here!" Mama yelled, trying to stand up, and Mama reached for the knife she'd been using to peel the potatoes. Daddy saw her too, the cold shine of the metal stopping him only momentarily

He grabbed her wrist and twisted it until the knife fell with an empty thump. Mama lost her footing as well. The potatoes on the floor rolled everywhere, and the water on the stove boiled over. I bolted to the door to get help. I couldn't take on Daddy myself.

"Don't go nowhere, girl," he said, his voice possessed by the whiskey. "It's time you learned what happens to women who don't know their place!"

Daddy slapped Mama again. "This is what you wanted, isn't it!"

I turned away, crying, so I didn't see the rest. I heard Mama's agonizing screams, and then silence. The only sound was what unspeakable act was happening in the corner, and my sobbing. Mama lay limp on the floor, her arm turned at a horrible angle, bone and blood showing. Her lips, red with blood, were opened, wordless—her eyes, staring at nothing.

I turned to run when Daddy grabbed me. His eyes bored into mine. "Where are you goin'?" he slurred, the liquor overtaking him.

I froze in fear. His hand lightly stroked my face as I looked at him in horror. His breath reeked of whiskey, and the smell of Mama. "You look like she used ta," he murmured, "when she was still fine."

Terror gripped me until I thought I was going to faint. "Please, Daddy, don't," I whispered.

At the sound of the word 'Daddy', he stopped. He seemed to wake from a trance, and he stepped back. He looked past Mama, passed out on the floor, her dress still over her hips, her nakedness exposed, her arm in that grotesque angle.

"Finish cookin' dinner," he growled at me and slammed the door on his way out.

I ran over to Mama, pulled down her dress, and tried to wake her. It took a long time. I sat there on the floor, cradling her head, with a kitchen towel to stop the bleeding, and crying in the way of the insane. That's the way Billy found us, his bowl of blueberries forgotten. That was the last time I ever cried. I had no tears left.

October 1940

After Mama died, Daddy stayed with us and didn't go to that other woman's house. At least at first. He was too busy trying to feed us. He still found work on other people's farms, but it wasn't enough to even call it sharecropping. Most of the time, with the Depression on and all, he would get paid in food instead of cash money. If he picked corn at the Fuller's, they might pay him in four or five bushels of corn instead, or if he helped out at the Mayfield's ranch, The Lucky M, we might get lucky enough to get a side of beef or some ribs from a slaughtered cow. That was when Daddy stayed sober enough to work. Which wasn't much.

Billy was my older brother, three years older to be exact. We never looked much like brother and sister. I favored Mama, dark-skinned and brown-haired, my face frosted with freckles. Billy was huge, about six-four, but strong and lean from all the labor he did. He was built like Daddy in every way, almost as if Mama had nothing to do with his making. The girls at school often sighed when he passed by and flirted with him, but he didn't seem to notice. He was too busy trying to make up for Daddy's lack of support. Billy worked too hard, much harder than Daddy. He baled hay in the summer and fall, plowed fields, cleared land, and anything else he could find. And it wasn't easy, because there were plenty of grown men trying to find work. Billy's heart was solid gold, and he always put us first. Nothing was more important to him than making sure we were taken care of. He was more of a father figure than Daddy was. At age seventeen Billy was built like a man, and worked with the strength of two.

"Elizabeth, guess what?" He busted into the kitchen, fairly beaming.

I was doing the umpteenth load of laundry. Delilah couldn't wait more than an hour before she dirtied another diaper, and I was having trouble keeping up. I began to understand even more how hard Mama's life was. Jacob, a cute, but spoiled three-year-old, was constantly at my feet, demanding, needing, wanting. I couldn't help remembering that one time, a few years ago, that Mama had miscarried. I couldn't imagine having two more babies to take care of. I finish folding a tiny shirt before I replied, "What is it?" There, for now, the laundry bin was empty. Jacob ran around me asking for something to eat.

"Look," he said, and held out a wad of bills. It seemed impossibly big. I gazed in wonder at his grinning face.

"How in the world did you get this?" I asked, as I started counting the money.

"Oh, I was just running some errands for that new guy in town."

Billy! There's fifty dollars here!" I counted it again to make sure. "What did you do to get this? It must have been a lot of work."

"It wasn't bad. And you can go buy some groceries now! I know you were low, and Daddy's been drinking the money. We can hide them in the well house so he doesn't take them. I want you to go buy some fabric for a dress, too."

My eyes watered. I really did need a new dress. But how could I do that, buy things for myself, when I didn't know when we would see money again?

"I know what you're thinkin'," Billy began. "I don't want you to come home from the store unless you have dress fabric. No arguments!" He grinned again. His chestnut hair and green eyes made him almost identical to Daddy in looks, but not in heart. "Now go, get out of here." He picked up Delilah. "I'll watch Little Bit for now."

When I got to the general store, I was tired. I couldn't remember the last time I had slept for a whole night. Daddy never got up with Delilah when she cried, so I did. I went to the main counter and was greeted by Mr. Ferrell, the town grocer.

"Why, hello there, Miss Graham," he began. I was always a little wary of him. He always looked at me a little too long. "What can I do for you today?"

"Here's my list," I replied absently. I eyed some beautiful sky-blue fabric on display. I wondered how much it was.

"Will do," Mr. Ferrell answered. "Be right back," he said, and disappeared into the back storeroom.

Just then, the bell on the door clanged as another customer entered. I probably wouldn't have even looked over in that direction if I hadn't heard that voice.

It was Carolyn Clements, the woman Daddy was having an affair with. There was a beautiful brunette little girl, about two years old, holding her hand. She wore a lacy pink dress, with a matching bow in her hair to offset her ebony dark hair. On her feet were shiny black Mary Janes. She was fussing with her mother about something, whining and crying and generally throwing a fit. She plopped herself down onto the floor and began to really scream. Carolyn didn't see me at first, she was so distracted dealing with her daughter. She bent down to give her a swat, but the child was up and running toward me before she could get her.

"No, Mama!" she yelled. "No, no, no!" She circled around behind me, trying to hide. I turned and immediately recognized her emerald eyes, and her nose. She was the spitting image of Daddy.

"So sorry," Carolyn said awkwardly. She took the child out of the store, still kicking and screaming.

I left the store without buying anything.

Chapter 4

SAMANTHA

I was in a room of complete darkness. Then, in front of me, the lights on the stage came on and I realized I was sitting at a grand piano. There was not an empty seat in the house. I realized to my amazement, this was Carnegie Hall.

My dress, a beautiful emerald green gown, strapless and made of satin, fit me perfectly. My hair twirled around my head much like a crown, with delicate curled tendrils drifting down. I glanced down at the ivory keys and placed my hands on them. They felt like they always did. I took comfort in the familiarity of the piano, the way my hands knew what to do and how I didn't have to think. I started playing a song I had never heard before.

In the back of the theatre I heard a baby crying, first softly, then getting increasingly louder until I became so distracted I couldn't concentrate, and I started making mistakes. The crowd started whispering, then murmuring, but nobody did anything. Who brings a baby into Carnegie Hall? People started to turn around and point to the back of the theatre. I couldn't see much because of the stage lights. Finally, I stopped playing. It was futile. There was too much distraction. I felt panicky and scared.

I stood up from the piano and demanded, "Who has the baby?"

All of the audience seemed to be staring at a woman holding the howling infant.

The woman was me.

EMILY

Mom came home a few minutes ago. She told me that Sam had made it through the surgery. I was glad. I mean, we've had our differences and all, but that didn't mean I wanted her to die or anything. She's still my sister. Then, Mom told me Sam was pregnant. I'm shocked! She had told me not to tell anyone yet. Why would I? Why would I want to blab it all over school that Sam got herself knocked up?

That news couldn't have come at a worse time. I mean, I just got cheerleader last week! I knew Matt was bad news, and I knew Sam was probably doing stuff she wasn't supposed to, but I didn't think she had slept with him yet. I'm pretty sure that Sam was a virgin until she met Matt. Man, I didn't think I'd ever seen Mom so upset. On the one hand, I felt worried about Sam. On the other hand, I'm so embarrassed. Even when Sam screws up, she sucked up all the attention. I never thought Sam, Miss Honor Roll, Miss Julliard Candidate would be so stupid.

Right before Mom got home, Spencer left. He had been so great. He had stayed overnight here (Mom didn't know of course, she would FREAK) when Mom sat at the hospital with Sam. He'd been so sweet, so concerned for me and the family. He was the good one. Too bad for Sam she didn't meet him first.

Well, I guess it wouldn't matter, because Sam didn't really get along with Spencer. Probably the jealousy thing. One time I asked her why, and she just called him an idiot jock. Whatever. She was the only one that didn't like him. Mom loved him, and even Dad didn't mind me going out with him. He did things for Mom like fixing broken stuff or lifting heavy things, that sort of thing. The kind of stuff you needed a guy for. He even changed the oil in Mom's car last week.

Most of the girls at school drooled all over themselves

when he walked by. But that was as far as it went. He didn't even look their way. He was with me now. He didn't need anyone else.

EDEN

Finally, a shower. I turned up the water as hot as it would go. My skin seared under the spray, but I didn't care. I hadn't showered in about 36 hours. Nana said she would stay at the hospital and practically forced me to go home. I only left when she swore to call me if anything was new.

There is a bit of good news. I guess Sam's brain bleed wasn't as bad as they thought. It seemed to have resolved on its own. I was so grateful that Sam made it through even one more day. She was still on the ventilator, unable to breathe for herself. I spent most of the day there. I did everything for her. I bathed her, brushed her hair, and changed the pads under her when she went to the bathroom, which wasn't much. They were probably going to have to put her on a feeding pump today.

I was in the waiting room when Dr. Moore, the head neurosurgeon, came out in the green scrubs. His blond hair came undone underneath his surgical cap. His trimmed beard offset his chiseled features.

I noticed some blood on his scrubs. Blood, I knew, that had come from my child's veins. Robotically, I stood to shake his hand.

"Dr. Moore." I tried to speak, but the words were stuck in my throat, along with my tears.

His kind eyes looked at me with empathy. He motioned for me to sit.

He sat next to me on the ugly plastic chair. He didn't have to call my name when he came into the waiting room. We knew each other, at least on a casual basis. We had had many talks about our lives, sitting at the ICU desk at four in the morning. Well, that's not exactly true. I knew a lot more about him than he did about me. I knew about his divorce, his kids, his summer home by the lake. He knew what I wanted him to know about me, which is superficial. I didn't share a lot of my life with anyone here, except for Jennifer. I was there to work, not to blab my personal life to anyone who would listen. I tried to read his face, which he kept intentionally noncommittal-a perfect poker face.

"If she can make it through the next seventy-two hours," he said, "she has a good chance of making it. The pressure on her brain is relieved now. So that's one obstacle."

He stroked his beard and continued. "If you're going to ask me about whether she is going to be paralyzed or not, I still can't tell. Of course you know that."

His green eyes, the color of a rainforest, rested on mine. "Dr. Moore . . ."

"Please." His eyes met mine. "Call me Mike."

"Mike," I began, the word sounded foreign on my tongue. "What about . . .?" I couldn't even say it.

"Eden," he began, and paused for an agonizing moment. "Yes?"

"I don't know how, it shouldn't be, but the baby's fine."

I made a sound like a wounded animal, a primeval moan, and started sobbing. He held me until I stopped, which seemed like an eternity.

Chapter 5

ELIZABETH

I decided to hang around the hospital as long as my bones could take it, because Eden sure needed a break. I sat in the waiting room, listening to the sounds of the hospital. The overhead pages for different doctors, the sounds of the wheels of the gurneys, people talking on their cell phones as they rushed from place to place. The ding of the elevator, the sobbing of someone who had just gotten bad news, the joy of someone who had gotten good news, all blended together. I hoped we would soon get good news.

I went and sat by Sam's bed and held her hand for a while. I knew it wasn't visiting hours, and the nurse came in to tell me so, but when she saw me with Sam, she simply let the curtain fall back and didn't say anything. It was hard for her to boss around an old lady like me.

My heart broke when I saw how bad Sam looked. So many bruises and broken bones, the tube down her throat. She looked similar to the way I saw Diane last--broken.

That thought chilled me to the core.

EMILY

I was excited. Even though Mom would have liked us all to stay at the house, like there had been some sort of funeral, I wasn't doing it. Frankly, she was too tired to argue with me. Anyway, Spencer was coming over to see me. I tried on about nineteen outfits, trying to find the exact one that made me the prettiest. I decided on a chocolate-brown tank top, layered, with a red short skirt and pumps. I put the finishing touches on my makeup and straightened my hair until everything was perfect.

Spencer showed up exactly at six just as he promised. And he looked so hot. He'd gotten a new haircut, which made his hair look even better, and he wore a green polo and khakis. Man, did he know how to make even boring khakis look good.

I opened the door and greeted him with a kiss. Oh my god. He smelled so good, and he was clean-shaven. I really could have gotten into trouble there if I hadn't been careful.

"Hey, sweetie." He grinned at me with those perfect white teeth.

I swear, he couldn't be ugly even if he tried. He was born with those teeth! Me, I had to endure five years of braces to get my teeth to look right. He handed me a bouquet of pink roses, my favorite. I inhaled deeply and sighed, and then I realized he had another bouquet. I gazed at him quizzically.

"Oh," he said, kind of shyly. "I thought I might give these to Sam. Or you might give them to her for me, since she's in ICU and it's probably only family that can visit, right?" He looked at me for confirmation.

Really, could the guy get any more perfect?

"Yes, they only let family into the ICU," I explained. I was little miffed that I had to share roses with Sam.

Oh, well, if that's the rule," he said, appearing genuinely bummed.

"Yeah, that's pretty much the way it is. I haven't even been to visit her yet, because I'm not eighteen. Anyway, she's doing better now, Mom said," I told him, holding on to his hand. "Come in." I opened the heavy oak door to our living room.

I managed to locate a couple of vases and brought them to the kitchen sink for water. While I filled them, Spencer came up to me and put his arms around my waist. I felt dizzy and warm. Then, I felt his hot breath on the back of my neck.

"You're getting goose bumps," he murmured in my ear, and then I felt his fingers brush my hair off my neck and his warm lips there instead.

I moaned, feeling nothing but pure heat buzzing through my body. I put both of the vases into the sink, and without even turning the water off, I turned around and, hungry for his kiss, put my arms around his neck. His lips moved from my mouth to the hollow of my neck. It got harder to breathe. I was pressed up against the sink, and I could feel some of the water from the faucet on the back of my shirt, but I was barely conscious of it.

"Oh god, what are you doing to me?" he whispered in my ear. Then suddenly he said, "Is your mom home?"

"Yeah, but she's asleep. Don't worry!"

"Damn, Emily," he said, a little angry, "What if she found us?" He turned the sink off. He started to move away, but I stopped him by putting my hand beneath his shirt. I felt his hard chest, the firmness of his muscles. He was so beautiful.

"She hasn't slept in three days. Trust me, she's dead to the world."

"Wanna go to my room?" I asked.

He followed me like a lost puppy.

EDEN

I thought I wouldn't be able to sleep, but sleep I did.-Five straight hours. I only woke up because the phone was ringing.

"Hello?" I mumbled, trying to focus my eyes on the clock.

"Eden. It's Craig. What are you doing home? Are you sleeping?" He said *sleeping* as an accusation.

"What do you want?" I croaked. My eyes were grainy, and I felt a little nauseated. I was still so tired. I had been running on fumes for a couple of days, and finally even the fumes had evaporated.

"I'm at the hospital. That Dr. Moore was trying to find you." I could hear him exhaling smoke. "He almost wouldn't tell me anything about my own daughter, because he didn't know I was her dad. Can you imagine?" I had to smile. Yeah, I could imagine. "Anyway, for God's sake, Eden!" I could almost hear him running his fingers through his hair. "I think you should be here. What kind of mother are you?"

Okay, I was awake, and now totally pissed off.

"The kind of mother who just got home from the hospital six hours ago. The kind of mother that hadn't showered in three days, or eaten, and probably wouldn't have eaten unless Nana hadn't brought me any food. So screw yourself." I hung up the phone.

Seconds passed, then the phone rang again. No way was I going to do this all night. I picked up the phone. "Look, I told you to screw yourself!"

"Well, that's not very nice." I heard a familiar voice, but a voice that was not Craig's.

"Oh, crap." This followed a rush of panic as I sat up in bed. "What is it, Dr. Moore? Is Sam okay?"

"Oh, yes, she's the same. Nothing's happened."

"Oh. Okay. Well . . ." I was at a loss for words. "What did you need?" I thought I had filled out all the paperwork and stuff, but with being so upset, there was always a chance I forgot something.

"Uh . . ." He sounded uncomfortable. "I wanted to let you know, about five minutes ago I checked on Sam. She's resting peacefully. Your husband, Craig, told me he thought you were at home."

"Ex," I said automatically, closing my eyes.

"Sorry?" Mike sounded confused.

My voice sounded hoarse. I needed to get a drink of water or something.

"Craig is my ex-husband."

"Oh." I swear I heard him grinning! "Oh, well, he left that part out."

"I'm not surprised. Anyway, so she's the same? No changes?"

"If anything we're seeing signs of improvement. If she continues to improve, we're going to start trying to wake her up, so we can see if we can extubate her. I am not sure how well that's going to work."

"Oh, okay, I'll be right there."

"No, no. I'll wait till morning," he reassured me.

"Okay, well, I'll be there soon anyway." I was already locating my keys on the nightstand.

"Eden, don't." He was using his doctor's voice on me!

"Don't what?" I went to the bathroom and started running a brush through my hair. "Don't come down here. I've instructed the nurses to call me immediately if anything changes, and I will call you that very second. I promise." His voice softened.

"Oh, well." I felt at a loss. "I still need to get there. I don't want her to be alone."

So many times as a child I myself had been alone, and I didn't want that to happen to Sam.

"Eden, please, can you trust me?" he asked quietly.

I don't know. I hadn't ever really trusted a man in a long time.

"I want you to get some rest. Your grandmother returned as soon as your ex left. She's here with her, so Sam's not alone. Come in the morning about seven. I'll be here."

"Are you on call tomorrow morning?" I asked. It seemed strange. Dr. Moore, Mike, had been there all weekend. It should have been Dr. Bennett's turn. I really didn't like him. He was an ass.

"Don't worry, I'll be around," Dr. Moore answered. He acted a bit strange, but I was in too much of a fog to notice.

I headed back to my bed. "Okay, I'll get some sleep," I relented, my head already on the pillow.

"Good. Take care, Eden" As soon as he hung up, my eyes closed and I fell into a restless slumber, filled with disjointed nightmares about Sam.

Chapter 6

SAMANTHA

The breeze felt warm on my face. The sun, a soft kind of sun, not harsh or too bright, rose warm and comforting. I drifted through the wheat field, and even though I knew somewhere that the wheat should have been hurting my feet, chafing them, it wasn't. It felt soft, like - a million feathers.

Above me, a sky so blue it seemed impossible. A few puffy cottony clouds floated by. *That's what I'm stepping on*--the clouds. There was nothing there but me, the softly waving wheat, and the cerulean sky. I traveled for a long time, but I was without care. I was not hungry, or tired. I felt a pleasant sense of belonging, like I was supposed to have been there a long time ago.

The wheat had given way to soft green grass, the kind that grew after the first spring rain. In the air, I could smell it.-he scent of a hundred summers, of Fourth of July picnics, the salt air of the ocean, all rolled into one. In the distance I saw a piano. The same baby grand I was playing before.

I sat down on the polished black bench, and started to play. It was like before. I started playing a song I didn't know. I closed my eyes and let the music envelope me. The melody was sad and melancholy and left me with a feeling of wanting, a feeling of desire, of what, I didn't know.

After I'd played for what seemed like hours, I opened my eyes. I noticed that the sun hadn't moved. It was as if it was always morning, never night. Then I saw something I hadn't noticed before. A huge oak tree. Its trunk as wide as I was tall, and the leaves were a sparkling emerald green. The branches, more than I could count, reached up, stretching to the sky as if the tree and the heavens were lovers. It looked as if it had always been, and would always be.

As I gazed at the tree, I grew perplexed. I saw a beautiful woman in a long white summer dress, barefooted, swaying slowly back and forth on a swing that was tied to one of the branches. Her dress, the most brilliant white I had ever seen, stirred gently with the motion of the swing.

Her hair was a brilliant blond, the purest gold I had ever seen. It was soft and long and curled softly as it fell on her shoulders. When she swung, the strands moved ever so gently in the breeze. She was too far away for me to be able to discern more than that. I had to get closer. I had to see her, hear her voice.

My soul deep within me knew her, even if my mind didn't.

EDEN

Somewhere, far away, I heard something. It made an annoying sound, and it wouldn't stop. I realized it was the phone. *Why is Mike calling me back so soon? I thought he wanted me to get some rest*, I thought irritably.

I opened my eyes and glanced at the clock. Five o'clock in the afternoon! I had been asleep for four hours. I picked up the phone.

"Hello?" I answered somewhat groggily. The person on the phone was hard to hear, and I couldn't make out what he was saying. "Hello?" I repeated.

In the background, I heard a lot of noise, people talking quickly, somebody was yelling orders. I heard alarms going crazy.

The sounds of a patient dying.

EMILY

I couldn't believe it. Spencer and I finally had sex. I knew a lot of people said that the first time hurts, but it didn't. Spencer was unbelievably gentle. At one point, he gazed into my eyes, and that's when it happened. I had never felt quite like that before, waves and waves of pleasure. It was wonderful. We made love over and over, and each time was better than the last.

"Wow," I said, turning over and propping myself up on my elbow, and cozying up to Spencer. "That was amazing."

Spencer laughed. "Stop, you're going to give me a heart attack." He glanced at his cell phone and cursed. "It's five o'clock, Emily!" He jumped up and started putting his pants on. I kissed him once more before he went out my window. Just then, there was a knock at the door, and Mom was in my room.

ELIZABETH

I felt a bit hungry, so I got some Fig Newtons out of my purse. One of the nurses brought me a cup of coffee so I had something to drink.

"See, Samantha, I thought that Carolyn must have told Daddy about me seeing her in the store that day. It was almost as if Daddy felt that now that I knew about his other kid, the secret was out. He could come and go as he pleased. So he did.

"He wasn't bothering me like I worried he would. Since that day he touched my face, I had been worried he was going to try to hurt me. I never told Billy about that. I thought Billy would kill him. He was so enraged when he found us that day, and found me on the floor, trying to stop Mama from bleeding. He thought I cried because Mama was hurt. He didn't know what I knew, that Daddy had raped her and made me watch."

I continued to tell my story to Samantha, my beloved granddaughter. I was so mixed up over recent events.

On the one hand, I knew I should be angry about what happened to Mama, and what Daddy said to me later. But it seemed, for a while, that a part of me died that day. I couldn't feel anything. Not love, not hate, not fear. I stopped being afraid. I stopped praying. If God could let such a horrible thing happen to Mama, how could he protect me? What was the point anyway? It seemed like God, up in his heaven, didn't really care about what happened to people like us. He didn't care that Daddy did that to Mama, and had threatened to do the same thing to me, if I didn't behave.

Mama was never the same either. Something in her broke that terrible day. She still got up in the morning and made breakfast and washed the clothes, and tended to us, but there was an emptiness there. She did everything slowly. Mama's laugh, her joy, evaporated. She simply marked time. She had quit caring for herself, bathing, combing her hair, brushing her teeth. She was just shadow of who she used to be.

One day, I came in from hanging out the clothes, and I saw her, sitting in the rocking chair, slowly moving back and forth, back and forth, her eyes closed. The door was left open, and the breeze from the river blew in and cooled the house. It made a sad, sighing sound. My heart stopped for a moment. I thought she was dead. Then I saw her hands, the hands that always were quick to make a pie, or to reach for me to hug me, as they gripped the handles of the old rocking chair so tightly I could see the blood pooling around her fingertips. Her nails had not been cleaned in a long time, and the dirt was caked under them in layers. She hummed an old hymn, one I had heard before, but couldn't recognize it because Mama hummed in a minor chord, and it made the song so eerie I felt the hair raise on the back of my neck. I still hear that song in my nightmares.

I fell at her knees and took her hand. "Mama?" I said. She didn't respond. I patted her hands. They were still warm. "Mama, are you okay?" I started to shake her, to demand she answer me.

She opened her eyes then, but it almost scared me more, because they were empty windowpanes to a vacant house. She stared blankly ahead, ignoring my pleas.

I laid my head in her lap and whispered, "Mama, please come back. I'm gonna find a way to get us out of here, you and me. Billy, he can stay here and take care of the boys." She still didn't reply. "Mama, what Daddy did, that was . . . unspeakable. But I swear to you, I won't let it happen again. I'll kill him first." Rage sparked in my heart. I comforted it, fed it, and loved it. "Do you hear me, Mama? Do you believe me? We are going to get out of here."

Mama started to laugh.

I felt confused. I lifted my head and looked at her. She seemed crazy, detached.

"Mama?" I said, as I felt the familiar finger of fear clutch my throat. "Mama!" I shouted. "Stop it! Stop it! Do you hear me?" I demanded.

She stopped rocking and looked at me.

Her eyes began to seem more lucid, more lucid than I'd seen in days. For one second at least, her Indian eyes softened as she touched my hair. Her eyes drifted ahead again, and I almost gave up when I heard her say softly, "We can't get out of here, Elizabeth."

"Yes we can, Mama," I urged. "I've been thinking about it. I've saved some money from berry picking, and from washing Mrs. Ferrell's laundry." I rushed ahead, breathless to get it all said before she went away in her mind again. "I sent a telegram to Aunt Margaret in Tulsa. She says we can come live with her. Don't you see, Mama? We can start over. A whole new life." I rested my head on her lap and waited for her answer.

"Child, get this crazy idea out of your head this minute," Mama said in a voice that was not her own, wooden and dead, a hollow monotone.

I prepared to argue until I convinced her, but she stopped me cold with the words she uttered next.

"I'm pregnant," she said tonelessly. "I'm pregnant!" she shouted, and laughed again.

That laugh chilled me to the bone. I backed away from the cabin.

Mama alternated between the awful laugh and the sad, strange hymn. Terror engulfed me as I ran from the cabin. With the door open, I heard Mama's maniacal laughter almost all the way to the river. I ran and ran, even though it had started to sprinkle and the temperature dropped. All of nature around me seemed unnaturally alive.

There is a storm coming, the trees warned as their leaves shook in fear. *There is a storm coming*, the river said, as it foamed its waves in icy fear. *There is a storm coming*, the wind cried, and it blew an eerie tune in a minor key.

I knew I'd better get ready.

Chapter 7

ELIZABETH

I stopped going to school and started cooking and cleaning and taking care of Mama. Every day that her belly grew, her mind went further away. She grew unable to feed herself. Mama went to some dark faraway place and I couldn't find her.

I missed school, but what right did I have to think about that now, with Mama gone crazy and Daddy running off? The fact was I would probably never get to go back. But that was a distant concern. I worried about the food situation at home. We were running out.

Billy had made some money here and there, but it was sporadic at best. Was Daddy going to leave us there to starve?

When the situation seemed bleakest, God seemed to use Isabelle to get us through another day. Just when I looked in the empty pantry once again, willing food to appear, Henry, Isabelle's oldest son, showed up. I opened the door and saw him standing there with a sack of flour, some eggs and bacon, a bag of potatoes, and a jar of fresh milk. I couldn't open my mouth to say thanks, but I'm sure my eyes said it all. Henry brought the food inside and placed the items neatly on the table.

"Ma wanted me to ask you all if you wanted to come to dinner tonight," Henry said quietly.

I felt so overwhelmed I almost cried.

Wordlessly, Henry hugged me. We stood there for a long moment in the quiet of the cabin.

EMILY

Mom stopped short when she came into my room. Her eyes glanced suspiciously around. I could feel my breath quicken, my pulse race. Surely, Mom knew what happened here just a few minutes ago. Surely, she could smell the scent of sex in the air. Part of me wanted her to. Maybe she would finally see that she had more than one daughter. *I am here, too*, Mom… I looked into her eyes, willing her to see me, to notice me.

"We have to get to the hospital now," she said in a rush. "Sam's in trouble. She may be dying."

With that, she shut the door.

We didn't speak very much on the way to the hospital. Mom, even though her oldest daughter was possibly dying, did not run any red lights or stop signs. I felt a kind of panic rise up in my throat. What if Sam died? Would any of us recover? I think this was the first time everything felt real.

Mom parked the car and locked the doors. I followed her into the ICU. I had never been there, in all the years that Mom had been a nurse. The place frightened me. The nervous family members, speaking in hushed tones in the hallway, the smell of fear and burned coffee in the air, the anxious expressions on the other nurses' faces when they saw my mother, these were all foreign to me.

There was a lot of activity around the room at the end of the hall. People in scrubs rushed in and out of the room. Alarms screeched, hurting my ears. A tall man with blond hair and a goatee seemed to be in charge. He had the air of authority about him.

Finally, he stepped out of the room and found Mom.

"Eden, I think we have her stable for now." Mom sighed in relief. The man took her hand.

What was this? I eyed him suspiciously. Was he just being nice, or was he coming on to my mother? Mom seemed clueless.

Just then, Dad came in. He, too, saw the man holding on to Mom's hand. His eyes went from the man to Mom. He didn't notice me.

"What's happening?" he demanded.

That was a loaded question. It seemed to have more than

one meaning. The doctor noticed Dad's glare and dropped Mom's hand.

"I was just explaining to Eden that I think Sam is stable now. "We are running a few tests to make sure, but we think she's okay." He looked at Mom as he spoke, not at Dad. "Her oxygen saturation was dropping, even on the ventilator, which is not a good sign," the doctor continued. "I had to increase her SPO2 from 40% to 90% to keep her going. I'll watch her carefully and reduce it if possible. We need to try to get her awake more, so I've ordered that her sedation be decreased slowly. Once a patient has been resuscitated, their chances decrease significantly. It is still touch and go, and could go either way at any moment."

I couldn't help staring at the doctor, who so obviously had a thing for my mother. How sick was that? I mean, for god's sake, my sister was fighting for her life and Mom was in here trying to strike up a love affair with that old doctor. Sure, I guess he was good looking enough, but still. Not as handsome as Dad.

Ignoring them, I headed down the hall into Sam's room and saw her for the first time since the accident. Her head was bandaged heavily, her eyes closed. Her right arm and leg were in casts, and an I.V. pierced her arm. Different color bags hung from the pole, like ornaments on a Christmas tree. Nobody was in her room now. I sat in the chair next to her. I knew I wasn't eighteen but I didn't think anyone was going to throw me out. I watched my sister's chest move up and down and heard the hissing of the ventilator that she needed to keep breathing.

For the first time ever, I cried.

EDEN
December 1985
I still remember, like it was yesterday, December 22, 1985. The last day of school before Christmas break. The air had a chill to it, one that promised snow. My best friend,

Sarah Prior, and I walked home together, as usual, and she wanted to come over to my house for a while. She had bought a new Whitney Houston tape and we wanted to listen to it. I figured that today would probably be a good day for her to come over because Mom would be asleep. I knew she would because she and Randy (Oh gag me!) had been up late doing God knows what and she'd be sleeping it off. Otherwise, I would have never invited Sarah over. I was just too ashamed.

My life did not in any way measure up to hers. I could not tell her what my life was really like, life with Mama, because she was just a little too sheltered in her little *Leave it to Beaver* life to really understand. Plus, if she really knew what happened most of the time at my house, she probably wouldn't want to know me at all. But, I had seen the hurt in her eyes one too many times when she wanted me to invite her over and I pretended not to get the hint. I didn't want her to quit being my friend. Sarah and her family were the only good things in my life, and I didn't want to blow it.

Because I knew she wanted to come over, I had gotten up at five a.m. to clean the house. Most of the time, I was the only one who cleaned. Mom was usually too bombed to care, or not at home at all. I washed the dishes, and took our clothes to the laundry mat down the street. It was me who scrounged around in Mom's purse to find money to buy a loaf of bread, or a gallon of milk, or a package of bologna. Yesterday, when I looked in Mom's purse for money, I found two hundred dollars, in small bills.

My eyes widened at the amount of the money. The bills were wrinkled and dirty, but felt like heaven in my hands. Mom was usually too wasted to remember how much money she had, and if some went missing she never thought to blame me. One good thing about living with Mom was she never punished me for anything because she was never with it enough to know if I had done anything wrong. So she would not notice if I took ten dollars out of her purse.

Mom was bad with money. She didn't have a bank account or credit card, just loose cash.

I wondered where Mom got such a windfall, but I didn't ask too many questions. I took the money and bought some groceries. Instead of just cold cereal, I bought some eggs and bacon. I bought milk and bread and Pop Tarts. I bought some food for my cat, Garfield. Usually, like me, he just ate whatever he found, scraps I gave him. But that time, I bought him some Cat Chow.

If Mom were sober enough to ask where I got the money, I would just tell her Randy gave it to me to buy some beer for him. She'd believe that, even though the most money I'm sure Randy ever had was a couple of bucks, because, like Mama, when he got it, he immediately spent it on beer, or cocaine, or whatever. But Mom was so stupidly into Randy she only believed the best in him. Which, I admit, I used to my advantage to stay alive.

I was excited and anxious about Sarah coming over, and this time she wasn't going to let me off the hook. We got off the school bus laughing and chatting. I opened the front door with my key and did not see Mama. *Good*, I thought. *She is passed out in her room.*

Usually my routine after school worked something like this: I came in the front door, and the house was trashed. I went to the kitchen and made myself a snack, if needed. I checked on Mama, always knocking on the door first, just in case loser Randy was there. When I was satisfied she was okay, I did my homework, cleaned up a bit, and tried to make us something to eat.

I threw my book bag onto the table and told Sarah I'd be back in a minute. I knocked on Mom's door, and not hearing any protest, pushed it open.

Mama was not okay. She was passed out, half on the bed, half on the floor, her face beaten, her eyes swollen. I ran over to her and shook her. "Mom! Mom! Wake up!" I demanded.

She wouldn't wake up.

I panicked, because I saw a spoon and a lighter nearby, and a syringe on the floor, the kind of thing Mama used when she was doing heroin. I hid these under the bed. I put my ear next to her mouth, to see if she was breathing. Her breaths were shallow and far apart.

Sarah heard me calling Mama and stood at the door, looking stricken. I was angry then; angry at Mama for loving drugs more than me, angry at Sarah for forcing me to show her my life, angry at God for allowing that. Mostly, more than anything, I felt ashamed. Ashamed at my life, ashamed of Mama, ashamed at myself for hoping, for just a second, that I could be a normal teenager.

"Sarah, go tell your mom to call an ambulance!" I ordered, tears flowing down my face. If the ambulance came, our secret would be out. Mama might go to jail, or have to go to rehab. Where would I stay? Who did I have to ask? My chest felt tight, and the room spun.

Sarah's mom and dad came over immediately and stayed with me until the ambulance came. Joy held my hand and sat next to me on the couch. Bruce, who was an EMT, monitored Mama closely. A few minutes went by and he said, "She's not breathing."

I started crying, and Joy held me. It felt good to be held, to be loved, and, just for a moment, I pretended Joy and Bruce were my parents.

Bruce started CPR, alternating between compressions and breaths, compressions and breaths. A few minutes later I heard the ambulance outside and ran out to meet them. I waved them into the yard, and they quickly got their stretcher and some other supplies and went into the house. Since Bruce was there, I didn't have to say anything, until one of the men looked at me and asked me directly, "Does your mother do any kind of drugs?" The other man was on his knees, putting an oxygen mask on Mama's face.

"No," I lied, looking him in the eye. I figured they had tests for that kind of thing, and they'd find it anyway, but that didn't mean I needed to sell her out. If they found it, they found it.

The other guy started an I.V. on Mom, and they loaded her on the stretcher and put her into the back of the ambulance.

Bruce turned to me. "Come on, kiddo. You can ride with me."

Joy went back to her house to check on Sarah. Sarah had not come back since she went to find her parents.

Bruce had a new truck, a Ford Ranger, black. I climbed up into the cab and he started the engine. I could smell his aftershave and could see his tanned hands gripping the steering wheel. He was wearing a white T-shirt, and it fit tightly on his upper arms. Bruce was big into working out. He probably had to be to offset Joy's cooking. His profile was chiseled, and his face cleanly shaven. His dark hair was a little messy from doing CPR. I had never really noticed before, but he was a good-looking man. He shifted the gears fluidly and, I guess he felt me gaping at him, glanced at me.

"Listen, try not to worry." His voice kind as he reassured me. "Promise me you won't worry until you need to."

I nodded, feeling slightly flushed. He thought I worried about my mom, like I should have been. Really, I was admiring his arms.

I wore a jean skirt and white button-up shirt with the top with polka dots, the top two buttons undone, and a long fake pearl necklace. My shoes were blue flats. I always loved those shoes. I knew they weren't practical, but they were so pretty and I was always kind of a girly girl. I would spend an hour at least doing my hair and makeup in the morning. I had put my legs up on the dashboard and crossed my ankles. I hadn't realized, at first, because it was just a habit. That's how I always sat in our truck, back when Mama still had one.

I saw that Bruce had noticed my legs, and he turned away quickly. I saw his cheeks flush. I felt aware of myself then. I didn't feel like a little girl anymore. I could attract men like Mama. Maybe, I dared to hope, I would be prettier than her. I would certainly be wiser, because I would never drink or do drugs like she did. I would always have a clear head. I would always be in control.

For the first time that I could remember, I didn't do the right thing. I pretended not to notice he had looked at my legs and left them there, bare and long, up on the dashboard. I couldn't believe it, but I saw I was distracting him from driving, and at one point he almost ran a red light. I heard him curse, and I smiled secretly to myself.

Chapter 8

SAMANTHA

The emerald grass yielded to my feet, and after I passed through it looked the same, as if I was never there. I could see the woman more clearly now, and her pale skin had a sort of glow about it. Her entire body seemed to emit a soft light. She smiled at me, but did not step out of the swing. When I was finally next to her, we stood for a moment, our hair being played with by the same gentle breeze.

Her eyes were as green as the sea after a storm, and just as wise. Her fingers were long and graceful as she held on to the rope that tied the swing to the tree. "Hello, Samantha," she said, in a voice like gently moving wind chimes.

I saw a large rock, flat and cool, and I sat and gazed upon her. She was the most beautiful woman I had ever seen. Somehow, she seemed familiar, as if I had met her before, but I couldn't place her.

"Who are you?" I asked her, and held my breath, waiting for her reply.

EMILY

Sam had recovered, but I couldn't tell that she'd improved any. She still looked like a vegetable, not moving, not speaking. It was kind of creepy. I wanted her to wake up. I wanted her to be okay.

Spencer had been over a lot that week. Mom had been gone most of the time, because she barely left Sam at all. Dad showed up sporadically at the hospital, but he never thought to call me or check on me. Maybe it was selfish, but I needed him, too.

Spencer and I had slept together almost every day. With Mom not being there, and no school because of summer break, there was nobody to stop us. He was wonderful to me. Tonight, when he came over, I poured him a glass of Mom's wine. I drank one, too. It wasn't as if she would notice. We finished two glasses each, and I was feeling pretty tipsy by then. We were sitting on the couch, and Spencer started kissing me until I couldn't think.

"Emily, we can't keep doing that," he moaned. "You're so lovely, and it feels good, but we don't want anything to happen. I don't want you to get pregnant." His piercing blue eyes met mine.

"Don't worry," I said, kissing his neck until I felt him hard inside me once more. "I'm on the pill. I've been taking them for about six months, for problems with my period." I kissed him, my tongue tasting him, needing him.

"You don't have to worry," I repeated to myself. I felt dizzy from the wine and Spencer's body. "I won't be stupid like my sister."

All at once, I felt Spencer stiffen. He opened his eyes, and had a strange look on his face.

"What are you talking about? What about Sam?" he asked.

"Let's not talk about her right now," I said…

"What do you mean about Sam?" he asked again.

What in the world? I wondered.

"Sam's pregnant, the idiot." I giggled, unable to help myself after drinking so much wine.

Suddenly, there was a chill I couldn't deny.

ELIZABETH

The next year was full for me. Taking care of Delilah and Jacob, doing their laundry, trying to find something to cook with our dwindling supplies, took a toll on me. I was tired. It was the kind of exhaustion that never seemed to go away. Billy tried to help whenever he could, but he was spending more and more time with a guy he met. One day, he brought him over to meet me.

I had just brushed my hair and changed into a fresh dress when Billy came in with the stranger. "Elizabeth, this is Antonio Bettino. He moved into the Parker's place across the river. Antonio, this is Elizabeth, my sister."

I had never seen anyone like him before. He was not overly tall, probably a few inches taller than me, and slender. His hair was dark and wavy, a coalish black color, darker than midnight. His eyes were the same, dark as the bottom of the river. His skin was darker than ours as well, kind of a tan. He wore a nice suit, tailored to fit, a dark brown with a white shirt. He looked like he had money.

I suddenly felt very plain in my hand-sewn dress, my feet bare, my hands red from washing dishes and laundry all day long. He held his hand out for mine, which I shyly gave. My Indian/Irish skin appeared translucent next to his dark skin, and he lifted my hand to his lips. "It's my pleasure, Elizabeth." Then, to Billy, he said, "Billy, you didn't tell me your sister was such a beauty."

I felt heat crawl over my face.

"I didn't think I'd have to tell you," Billy bragged. "What's more, she is as smart as she is pretty." Antonio seemed impressed. "Sis, can Antonio stay for dinner? Do we have enough?"

My eyes met Antonio's and I smiled. "I'm sure I can make enough."

Antonio smiled back, his teeth as white as the clouds on the mountain.

EDEN

My days were full with being there for Sam at the hospital. I was there from the moment I woke up until the wee hours of the morning until I couldn't keep my eyes open anymore.

When I sat at her bedside, Nana was often with me. Worry etched across her ancient face, although she tried to hide it. Thank God for her. I always thanked God for her. It may seem sacrilegious to some, but Nana was my redeemer.

Chapter 9

SAMANTHA

"Samantha," the woman in white said, "I am here to tell you, to help you remember, and to make clear what has been distorted."

"I don't understand." I frowned. *What was she talking about?* I didn't know.

"Come, with me," she said, and I followed her, her cool white hand holding my own.

ELIZABETH

I wasn't sure what, if anything, was to be done with the information I had about Daddy. His other kid, I mean. Should I mention it to him, and ask for money? No, who would really care what Jonas Graham did? Nobody, that was who. In fact, I was surprised that Carolyn let him live with her, and her child. But she did. I guess it made sense, though. One of the few things Daddy was good at was making women fall helplessly in love with him.

So, for a few months at least, after Delilah was born, and Mama had been long gone, Billy and I were left to fend for ourselves. Nobody much cared about the Graham kids. Everybody had respected Mama, that was certain, but after the funeral and Daddy dragged in late looking like he did, well, we didn't get many visitors. We were the poorest white trash on the mountain, everybody said so.

Occasionally, Isabelle would come over with a loaf of bread and a bowl of soup, or a layer cake with a pound of tea. Isabelle didn't have much to spare either. She had five kids of her own:

Henry, who was 17; Danny, who was 14, and the biggest idiot I ever saw, by the way; Virginia, who was 10; Faith, who was 8; and Margarite, who was 5. So she had her own troubles, her own problems, her own mouths to feed. I could read the worry in her eyes when she stopped by occasionally to check on us. I would lie about where Daddy was, lie about how we were doing, lie that I was fine. I could tell Isabelle didn't really believe me, but she was hesitant to do anything of real consequence. I knew that Mama had been too proud to tell Isabelle about how harshly Daddy treated her. I didn't think that Daddy treated Carolyn that way. I hated her, too, her honey-blond hair and perfect figure that had turned Daddy's eye from Mama, from us.

I thought that David, Henry's dad, said something to Daddy because he started to come around more, about once a week, with food or money, or a deer he had killed, that sort of thing. I didn't speak to him, nor he to me. I couldn't look at him after what happened. I could not bear to see his eyes, and I was afraid of him, and his threat.

One morning, I was putting a mock apple pie out on the windowsill to cool. My hair was in a French braid, and it had grown down even past my waist. The heat was getting to me that afternoon, especially with the baking. The summer sun beat down on the dirt road in front of the cabin, heating the soil and causing waves of humidity to rise from the ground. The trees on the mountainside were green and expectant. In fact, the mountain looked choked with greenery, and the river foamed brownish from all the leftover spring rain. It swelled at its banks menacingly, frightening even in its beauty. From the front porch of the cabin, I could see the river, and even hear its rushing outside of my window at night.

Mr. Ferrell, the storeowner, came up the path to our house. Something in me stiffened. I knew this couldn't just be a social visit.

"Mr. Ferrell?" I asked, wiping my hands on my new apron. I had sewn it from the material that Billy had bought me at the store. That day when I saw Carolyn and her daughter, and came back home so upset, Billy immediately went back to the store and bought the fabric for me. He bought so much of the sky blue fabric, not knowing how much I needed. I had enough to sew a dress, an apron, and a tiny dress for Delilah. She looked so cute in it.

"Afternoon, Elizabeth." Mr. Ferrell peered around with his ferret-like eyes. He was a fat man, and insisted on wearing a suit even on the hottest days. I always thought he just wanted to flaunt his so-called status as the richest man on the mountain. That day he wore a white suit with a starched white shirt and navy tie. His huge belly, domelike, protruded over his pants and pressed at the buttons holding his shirt tight. His beard, white as snow, and trimmed neatly. His round glasses gleamed in the afternoon sun. "Is your daddy around?"

I sighed. "No, he isn't. What is it that you need?"

His eyes were leering at me, coming to rest on my breasts. I crossed my arms across my chest defensively.

"Need to speak to him." He glanced at his pocket watch, then snapped it shut just as abruptly, as if to emphasize how busy he was.

"What is this concerning?" I leaned over the porch rail.

His cheeks appeared flushed with the May heat. Summer came early in the mountains. "He owes me money. I gave him a loan a few months back for supplies, and he hasn't paid. I'm gonna be needing that money today, if possible."

"Well, I don't know what to tell you. He isn't here. You could try over at Miss Carolyn's. You know he stays over there quite a bit."

He had the decency to blush at the mention of her name. There used to be rumors that before Daddy came on the scene, he used to frequent her house quite a bit himself.

"I'm not in the habit of tracking down people with bad debts." He lifted his chin condescendingly. "He owes me twenty dollars."

I gasped. There was no way Daddy could pay that back. (In the thirties, twenty dollars was about the same as two hundred now, which, to us, might as well have been two million.) Daddy didn't have a regular job to begin with, just bits of sporadic work here and there, and not enough apparently that he wanted to share any of it with us. The men that lived by the river didn't want to hire Daddy. He was lazy and unreliable, and their wives flirted with him. I suspected that when Daddy did have a few dollars not allocated to whiskey, he spent all his money on Carolyn and that daughter of hers.

Mr. Ferrell took his handkerchief out of his pocket and wiped his bald head. "You tell your Daddy, when you see him, to come see me. I'll give him another week." I tried to seem unconcerned, but was having problems doing so with the way that he was blatantly leering at me. "I'll be back here then."

I stared at him levelly. "I'm sorry Daddy didn't pay you, but I can't do anything about it. Frankly, I think it was foolish of you to loan him that money in the first place." I lifted my chin, my stubborn pride showing once again.

"Maybe so, maybe so," he repeated, still studying me slowly up and down. "If your Daddy don't pay," he said, his eyes resting on my breasts again, "maybe you and me can work out somethin'." He licked his lips.

I felt like I vomiting. "Shouldn't you check with your *wife* on that one?" I asked, my hands on my hips. I wasn't about to whore myself out for my daddy's debt. He chuckled a little at that one as he turned to leave. He turned to me and said, "Don't worry, I don't mind the ones that got a little spirit in 'em." Then he left down the road, whistling to himself.

EDEN

Mama was going to be in the hospital for a while. She was pretty beat up. For some reason, she hadn't taken any drugs that day. She was plenty drunk, but the heroin stuff was not hers. Who knew that straight-laced accountant types like Julian could do drugs too? Anyway, because there was no drug use, and Julian sat in jail, there wasn't going to be any social worker coming to take me away from Mama. I still could not get over the fact that Julian, the man I had hoped would be my dad, was every bit the sleaze as Randy, if not more. Randy had never hurt Mom like that. I knew that my life was screwed up living with her, and sometimes dangerous and almost always unhappy, but I loved her and wanted to stay with her.

For the time being, Joy said I should stay with them until Mama felt better. So every day after school, I would ride the bus home with Sarah. I got to sit around the table and eat dinner with them. Dinner at their house was a study in contrast to dinner at our house.

Most of the time, Mama would be passed out on the couch, or gone altogether. I would sit in front of the television, watching something mindless while I heated up whatever was left in the fridge. But when I stayed with Sarah, I pretended her family was my real family. Sarah was my sister, Joy was my mom, even Sarah's kid brother, Cody, was okay. Sure, he was bratty, but not any brattier than the little brothers on the *Brady Brunch* reruns or my favorite show, *Growing Pains*.

Even though I thought of Joy, Sarah, and Cody as family, I felt something quite different for Bruce. I was not like most teenage girls, giggly and obvious. I had grown up quickly with Mama, and had been paying attention to the way she attracted a man. Unconsciously, Mama's ways came to me. I never purposely did anything, at first. It was like that day when I rode over to the hospital with Bruce and put my legs up on the dashboard. I'd done that a million times before with Mama. I just didn't realize at first what effect I could have on a man, until I'd noticed Bruce's embarrassed reaction when I caught him ogling at my legs. The difference, if I was to be honest with myself, was that I would do something unconsciously, then, after I noticed how it affected him, I would pretend not to notice, and kept doing it. It made me feel powerful in a childish way.

One day, Bruce stayed home from work. He had picked up the stomach flu from Cody and had been awake most the night throwing up. I had the same thing, and was just as sick. Joy insisted I stay home as well. She drove the other kids to school. Bruce stayed in bed and did not come out all morning.

I was not feeling too hot. I had a fever earlier, and then I got the chills. I could not get myself warm. I decided to get in the shower. I turned up the water as hot as I could take it, using some of Sarah's rose-scented body wash. I stayed there a long time. Finally, I got out of the shower and reached for a towel. I put my left foot on the side of the tub and dried myself off. I had started to dry my hair when Bruce opened the door. I usually locked the door, but that day I had forgotten.

I froze. I didn't even grab the towel to cover myself. I just held my hands to the towel pressed to my hair. Bruce stared, his mouth open in shock and embarrassment. His eyes started traveling the length of my body. I took my foot off the tub, and stood facing him.

I realized at that moment, I should cover myself, but I didn't right away. Instead, I dropped the towel onto the floor, pretending it was an accident. I slowly bent over to pick it up, making sure that he noticed every movement. My body was still glistening from the shower. I pretended to be startled and covered myself quickly. Bruce finally woke up and shut the door.

I finished drying myself, smiling the whole time. For some reason, I didn't feel sick anymore.

Chapter 10

SAMANTHA

It was springtime and everything was in bloom. I could hear music, soft and melodic. When I listened closer, I could tell it was an old Judy Garland song.

Then I smelled the roses. Roses of different colors: deep reds and pastel pinks, snow whites and lemon yellows bloomed and climbed up the trellis of a yellow clapboard house on the side of the road. Wild lavender stretched across the sides of the road, and there was a white picket fence surrounding the yard.

In front of the house was a large table covered with a white linen tablecloth. A dozen chairs of different styles and shades were seated around the table. A clear glass bowl with assorted lilies sat in the center of the table. White candlesticks in brass holders were placed elegantly, and the brass napkin rings match.

A slight breeze touched some wind chimes, singing a sad melody. The woman stopped in the yard and did not go closer.

Another woman, long and lean, wearing a baby pink summer dress stepped out in the yard. Her blond hair was piled high on her head and she was wearing a string of pearls. She was holding a box of silverware and began to place them on the table. A dark-haired man came out onto the porch. He was handsome and tanned and was wearing a pressed white buttoned-up shirt and coal gray slacks and socks that were the same color. His shoes were black and looked expensive. He was trying to tie his tie.

"Babe?" he asked, and the woman turned to him with the smile of a lover.

"Ah, having some trouble?" she asked him. She put the box of silverware onto the table and went to him. She moved like a dancer. Even something as common as walking a few steps seemed like poetry when she did it. She climbed up the steps and put her thumbs lovingly under the part of the tie by the back of his neck. Instead of tying it, she used it to pull him to her lips. They kissed passionately for a few minutes, and she led him into the house, the tie forgotten.

ELIZABETH

The rest of the week, I worried about Mr. Ferrell coming back. I figured he would, once he decided how Daddy's debt was to be paid. I never thought about calling the police, because in War Eagle, Mr. Ferrell's brother, the sheriff, was the law. Mr. Ferrell was right about one thing, nobody would believe him over me. The Grahams were Irish-Cherokee trash, and everybody knew it.

I knew Daddy wouldn't pay him. He had no sense of honor about anything, much less a feeling of responsibility for paying bills. Mama wasn't there to pay them anymore, and I suspected that Carolyn took care of his expenses there. She had saved money over the years in her business as a prostitute, and so, at least by War Eagle standards, she was wealthy. I sometimes wondered how long she would be wealthy with Daddy under her roof. I was sure that he would squander all of her money and have nowhere else to go.

I noticed a small figure at the end of the dirt road by our house. I squinted in the harsh Arkansas sunshine, and couldn't tell who it was at first. As he moved closer, I realized it was not Mr. Ferrell or Isabelle. It was that Italian man, Antonio. Billy was not with him.

As he neared the house, I noticed he was wearing a white short-sleeved button-up shirt and navy blue slacks. He had wisely decided not to wear the jacket he usually did. Even though he was warm from the midday heat, I was startled by the raw sex appeal of him. His tanned arms, not hidden in a jacket, were muscular and firm. His dark hair was a bit disheveled, but even the messiness of his hair becoming uncombed had a rakish appeal. I felt my heart quicken in a way I had never experienced.

I usually did not have time for love affairs, especially not now. Whenever I was not doing some sort of household chore, I spent my time reading books. They had been my first love. I had a silly dream that one day I might write books for a living. That was an impossibility with me trapped in this cabin on the mountain.

Antonio waved and smiled.

I shyly waved back.

"Hello, Elizabeth," he called in his beautiful accent.

"Hello, Mr. Bettino. What brings you here today, out in this heat?" He was close enough to the porch that I could see the few drops of sweat on his forehead.

"Call me Antonio. Mr. Bettino is my father." He grinned at me.

My face heated. Something about him made everything I said somehow seemed like an embarrassment.

Antonio moved closer to the foot of the porch and wiped his brow with his handkerchief.

I noticed a gold watch, heavy and expensive, on his handsome wrist. A drop of sweat had settled on the top of his upper lip, and I had a crazy urge to taste the sweat on my own lips. Shocked at my thoughts, I blushed, thinking surely he could read my mind. I felt furious at my foolishness.

"Do you have anything cool to drink for a weary traveler?" He grinned again.

God, that accent. I swear he could have said "pass the peas" and it would sound sexy.

"Oh, sure," I replied, feeling flustered. It was not like me to be so unsure about myself. Something about the way he looked at me made me feel like he could see right through me.

I poured him a glass of lemonade and he sat next to me on the porch. Finally, I had to ask.

"What are you doing here?" Then, I felt kind of embarrassed for sounding so rude. Mama would have never talked this way to anyone.

Antonio raised his eyebrows. "Well, I guess I could always leave if I was unwanted." I noticed him staring at my lips. That was distracting. "You don't have to leave. I was just wondering. I mean, nobody comes here to see us unless it's bad news." I noticed his black eyes, dark as the caves down the river. "I mean no offense," he began as he took a long sip of lemonade, "but most of the people in this town are not exceptionally brilliant." He grinned at me again. "Except for you, Elizabeth. You have a wonderful mind."

"And how have you come to this conclusion?" I asked, feeling electricity between us. I could tell he did too.

"The way you speak, for one. You sound educated. Also, I have noticed your books. So many books! So many different writers. Aristotle and Tolstoy, Hawthorne and Crane, Dickens, Twain and Austen. I saw *The Iliad* sitting in your kitchen, for heaven's sake!" He gawked at me, impressed.

"I like to read. This doesn't mean I'm brilliant."

"Really? I'd like you to show me one person on this mountain that even knows who Poe is."

I had to laugh at that. He was right. Most of the people on the mountain had little schooling past sixth grade. Pa couldn't even read at all.

"I do have a question, though," Antonio said. "Who is Aubrey De Vere?"

I was surprised. I was unsure how he had come up all of this information about me and my books. He must have asked Billy, but why?

"He's an Irish writer, my favorite poet," I said.

"Your favorite poet, huh?" Antonio took out a cigarette and lit it. "Prove it."

"Prove it? What do you mean?" He was so confusing.

"He's your favorite poet. So quote something."

The only poem I could seem to call to mind was one of his love poems. This could be a problem!

"Uh, well . . ." I stammered.

"Come on, you know you know one of her poems. Tell me." He smiled, and I went weak.

"All right. Well here's one my grandmother loved. It's called 'The Mighty Mountain Plains.'

"The mighty mountain plains have we two trod
Both in the glow of sunset and sunrise;
And lighted by the moon by southern skies
The snow-white torrent of the thundering flood
We too have watched together: in the wood
We too have felt the warm tears dim our eyes
While zephyrs softer than an infant thighs
Ruffled the light air of our solitude.
O Earth, maternal Earth, and thou O heaven,
And Night first born, who now, e'en now, dost waken
The host of stars, thy constellated train,
Tell me if those can ever be forgiven,
Those abject, who together have partaken
These sacraments of nature—and in vain?"

Antonio had closed his eyes as I recited the poem. When I finished, he opened his eyes and looked at me admiringly. I felt embarrassed by the expression on his face.

"Irish poetry? Who knew it was so beautiful? I guess we Italians don't have the corner market on the arts."

We sat on the porch silently for a few more minutes, listening to the roar of the river and the sounds of the birds in the bush behind us.

Suddenly, Antonio spoke. "Elizabeth, I'm here because I want to ask your permission to court you." I breathed in sharply, stunned. Nobody had been interested in me before. Well, nobody with noble causes. Antonio, who I guessed to be twenty-five or so, was interested in me, a seventeen-year-old hill girl? Why?

I remembered my vow to myself about not letting any man control me. I could see myself losing myself to Antonio. I had a sudden memory of Mama, lying on the floor of the kitchen, her arm broken and bleeding, almost dead.

Suddenly angry, I stood up and leaned on the porch rail, my arms crossed. I don't know what you've heard, but I'm not easy like most of the girls in this town. And just because my daddy's living at a whore's house doesn't mean I'm a whore as well. So if you're looking for an easy lay, you might as well go down the street and talk to Mary Jones. I've heard she puts out." I took a drag from my cigarette, then glared at him directly.

In an instant, Antonio rose to his feet and was standing across from me, his hands on my shoulders roughly. For a second, I was afraid. Was he going to be like Daddy, and push me around? It wouldn't surprise me. I challenged him with my icy stare.

"Damn it, Elizabeth! I'm not your father." With that, his lips were on mine.

I felt a shiver running through me. His hands were in my hair, on my neck, on the small of my back. He kissed me until I couldn't see straight, his tongue meeting mine. Then, he backed off, breathing heavily. He ran his lovely fingers through his ebony hair. "Elizabeth, I'm a gentleman, and I'll prove it to you. But something about you brings out the beast in me."

And with that, he was gone.

I was left standing on the porch, watching him angrily stalk off. I touched my lips, bruised where he had kissed me, and wondered if I would see him again.

EDEN

After the incident in the bathroom, things got really weird really quickly between Bruce and me. I could tell he was worried about being alone with me. I found that extremely amusing, and somewhat empowering. I certainly didn't try to invent circumstances that would place us alone together, but the strange thing was, opportunities seemed to happen all the time. I felt a little guilty, because I knew that Joy left us alone together because she trusted us. Or maybe, the more likely reason was it never occurred to her that something might happen between Bruce and me. After all, I was just a child, right?

Mama was in the hospital for several weeks. When she was stable enough to move out of ICU, she still had a long way to go. She had been beaten so badly that she required four surgeries and months of physical therapy before she was ready to go home. The horrible thing about it was, I didn't really feel sorry for her. I mean, it's not as if I wanted Julian to beat her up or anything.

One day, Joy told Bruce to take me to the hospital to visit my mother. Based on his expression, I could tell he was obviously searching for a way out of it. However, he couldn't think of a good enough reason, and Joy was clearly becoming annoyed.

"Bruce, come on," she said, as she stirred the spaghetti sauce. "I'd take her, but I'm right in the middle of cooking dinner. You don't mind, do you?" Bruce sighed and shook his head.

He looked my way and said, "Meet me in the truck in the ten minutes."

I changed quickly into a clean blouse that Mom had bought me once but I never wore. When I studied myself in the mirror, I realized how low cut the blouse was. I had never worn it because I felt uncomfortable showing that much flesh. God knows it didn't bother Mama. She was always telling me to not be afraid of being a woman. "If you got it, flaunt it," her voice echoed in my head.

The blouse was a sky blue that made my eyes seem even bluer. I put a denim jean jacket over it so it wouldn't be as obvious. I brushed my hair quickly and changed into a skirt that showed off my legs, and put on a pair of red flats.

I glanced in the mirror again and realized I was not exactly dressed to see my mother in the hospital. I was dressed as if I was going on a date with Bruce. I spritzed on a little of my mother's perfume that I had taken from her bathroom.

Bruce was scraping the ice from the truck windows when I stepped outside. When he saw me, he stopped for just a second. I knew he noticed me. He had an irritated expression on his face and went back to scraping.

I got into the truck and shivered because the heater was not warmed up yet and the vinyl seat was cold on my legs.

Bruce climbed in and started the engine. He glanced at my legs, then looked away. He seemed angry.

"Eden," he said, gripping the steering wheel, "do you really think that outfit is appropriate to go visit your mom in?"

The cold tone in his voice immediately made me furious.

"My mother bought this outfit for me."

"Oh, well, *that* figures," he mumbled, putting the truck into gear.

"What's that supposed to mean?" I asked. "What are you trying to do, be my father?"

"No," he said in almost a bitter chuckle, "but God knows you need one." He lit a cigarette before he drove out on the highway, sort of recklessly.

"Geez, do you have to drive so crazy?" I yelled, and grabbed on to the dashboard for dear life. "There's still a lot of ice on the road from the storm last week," I reminded him.

"What are you, the Weather Channel?" he said in a snotty voice, as he shifted the truck into fourth gear. "I think I know how to drive."

"Yeah?" I said, and because of the lack of anything else to say, I added, "Well, I don't." I crossed my arms and stared out the window to the trees frosted with ice. Some of them appeared impossibly heavy, the weight of the ice forced their branches to the ground. The ice gave the trees sort of a fairyland effect. God knows my life was not a fairy tale. Even the trees were mocking me. The weight of my life, like the ice on the trees, weighed me down.

"Really?" he said, blowing smoke from his lips. "Doesn't your mother drive?"

The truck's heater was finally doing its job, and I held my fingers up to the vents to warm them.

"Are you kidding?" I snorted. "My mama's too busy with her drugs, her booze, and her men, to teach me much of anything."

He didn't say anything else and he just turned on the radio. Prince was crooning "Raspberry Beret."

I gave Bruce a sideways glance and asked him, "Aren't you going to change the channel?"

"Why?" Bruce asked, thumping his fingers on the steering wheel.

"Well, Joy always does. Don't you like country like she does?"

"No, I can't stand any of that twangy crap." He stopped the truck to wait at a red light. He took another drag from his cigarette and then spoke again. "Joy, she's a good woman, you know that. She likes different things than I do. You know, she's ten years older than me?" he asked. "Sarah is Joy's daughter from her first marriage. She never told you that?"

"No, she didn't. So how old does that make you? Fifty?"

He roared with laughter. "You are a harsh little girl. No, I'm twenty-seven." He looked at me with his warm brown eyes.

"Well, I'm not a little girl," I said, holding my chin up. I crossed my legs for good measure.

Bruce pretended not to notice. "No, you're not," he said quietly.

There was an awkward silence for a moment, and the light turned green. The truck lurched into motion. "I can't believe Sarah never said anything about you not being her dad. Cody is yours, though, right?" I asked.

"Yep, Cody is mine." He grinned. "Couldn't deny him even if I wanted to."

"That's so weird. I guess I just always assumed . . ." I started to say. He parked the truck in the parking lot of the hospital. "Do you know what they say about assuming?" he asked, and leaned over so close to me I could smell his aftershave and see the start of a five o'clock shadow on his jaw.

I swallowed, totally engulfed by the pure maleness of him. "What?" I croaked. I could feel his breath, hot on my neck.

"Don't," he said simply, then he put the brake on and exited the truck.

It took me a moment to catch my breath.

EMILY

I wasn't sure what had happened between Spencer and me, but something had. It seemed like he had been avoiding me. He just wasn't himself. He was coming over that night. I hoped we could talk about whatever was bothering him. I was worried he was planning to break up with me.

I put on my shortest skirt, my camouflaged kami with my sexy strapless bra underneath and left my hair down. As usual, Mom was at the hospital. I hardly saw her anymore.

The doorbell rang. I let Spencer in and went over to the couch. "Hey, baby," I said, and patted the couch next to me.

He came over reluctantly, it seemed, and sat next to me. Then, he turned on the football game! I sat quietly for a moment and then started kissing his neck.

"Sorry, Em." He sighed. "I'm not in the mood today"

I didn't believe him. He was always in the mood. Or else, he used to be.

"What's wrong?" I asked, twirling his gorgeous blond curls between my fingers.

"Does anything have to be wrong?" He turned the football game up.

Desperate times call for desperate measures. I started teasing him, flirting.

He shuddered. "Emily, really . . ."

But he couldn't help it. He couldn't resist me. And, if only for a moment, it was just the two of us in the world.

Chapter 11

SAMANTHA

As quickly as I saw the house in the country, the woman wanted to move on. We proceeded further down the country road for what seemed like miles.

"What is your name?" I asked the woman shyly. She was so beautiful it was like talking to a goddess. I was afraid to meet her eyes directly. Something inside me was terrified that to do so would be like seeing the surface of the sun.

"My name is Delilah." She hummed a song.

It was an old one, but I recognized it from somewhere. I thought it was an old sixties song. It seemed out of place there in the wild country, but when she sang it, it somehow seemed to fit, like a piece of a puzzle that could be forced to work even though it shouldn't.

Delilah. Where had I heard that name? It seemed just on the edge of my memory. I knew it, as I knew her, but I could not seem to grasp it. It was like trying to hold a piece of melting ice.

"Where are we going, Delilah?"

The road was steeper now, and harder to navigate. Although it was rocky and winding, I never hurt my feet or cut my skin on the jagged rocks. The dense vegetation sometimes seemed to threaten to overwhelm us, but it didn't. Honeysuckle bloomed wildly along the side of the road, and its fragrance was sweet and thick. The trees and bushes that grew on either sides of the dirt road seemed so packed and choked that it seems to be a miracle that they were able to get enough water, but somehow they did.

Delilah didn't answer me, and I realized she was not going to.

After what seemed like hours, we were at the top of the mountain. The trees, pines and oaks, sugarberry and walnut, were gloriously tall, and they seemed hundreds of years old. A clear mountain stream gurgled past, in no a hurry to get somewhere. The sky was a light baby blue, and soft puffy clouds lazily floated back and forth. The earth was an emerald green as well, a soft carpet of clovers.

I thought I saw what she wanted me to see.

In front of me a young boy, about ten or so, struggled behind a bulky plow. It was difficult for him to manage the unruly mule, but he was working hard. His dark hair was matted to his face, and sweat poured down his forehead. His dirty face was weary.

He wore a white shirt that had been hand sewn and brown trousers, the trademark clothes of a sharecropper. His work boots seemed too large for his feet. He finished the row, paused for a moment, then wiped his brow in the noonday heat. Who knew how long he had been out there working? His clothes were soaked with perspiration.

Rows and rows of torn earth, too many to count, had been plowed today. Had the boy done it all himself? Where was his help? From where I was standing, I could see the cuts on his hands that were bleeding profusely.

The noonday sun beat down relentlessly on him. He appeared dizzy, but had no time to rest. There was too much work left to do. For each row he had plowed, there were three more still to plow.

Suddenly, I could see a man in the distance marching quickly toward the boy. He seemed angry, and although he trudged along at a brisk pace, he weaved occasionally, as if drunk. The boy did not see or hear the man coming, but I felt a lump of panic come up in my throat. I had to warn the boy. I started yelling at him, trying to get his attention, but I couldn't seem to. Tears welled up in my eyes when I realized there was no point to my trying to call to him. He couldn't hear me.

The man, tall and looming, his shadow impossibly long, quickly overtook the boy. The boy immediately tried to start plowing again, but it was too late. The man had seen him resting.

"Boy! What are you doin' out here, slacking this way?" The man seemed to have an Irish brogue about his words. Without waiting for the child to reply, his fist came down heavy on his head.

I gasped in anguish.

The boy crumpled like a fragile piece of paper.

"Pa! Please, I was just . . ." The boy, not crying, tried to explain.

"Don't give me excuses, boy! You know you were supposed to be workin' out here, not daydreaming the morning away. *Look at this*!" He impatiently waved toward the part of the field that was unplowed. "Ya should have been done with more than this, that's for sure and certain!"

"But, Pa, I'm thirsty, and hungry," the boy pleaded.

"Here, have a sip." With that, he gave the boy a flask.

What was in there, alcohol? It must have been because the boy drank deeply from the bottle, then coughed profusely. The boy began crying.

The man used the flask to hit the boy across the face. The boy fell into the dusty earth.

"I told ya, men don't cry!" The man, red-haired and pale and enormous, finished off the flask and put it back into his pocket. He eyed the boy with disgust, then kicked him in the ribs.

I cried out in horror, but the boy had stopped crying, audibly anyway. His tiny body remained still on the dirt, as though he was afraid to get up.

"I'll be back here in one hour, do ya hear me? And when I do, there better be a lot more done. If it looks good, you can eat then."

The man wavered back toward the tiny farmhouse in the distance, where a small, dark Indian woman was hanging laundry on a clothesline. She was petite and slender, although the dress she wore was too large for her. Her husband spoke to her, and I couldn't hear the conversation anymore, but she saw the boy in the field and became upset. The man went into the shack and within seconds she was flying across the field, running barefoot, her dark ebony hair falling down from the bun.

She knelt at the boy's feet, crying now, and tried to turn him over, but he moaned in pain. She gasped in shock at the boy's bloody nose, the crimson liquid mixed with the layers of dirt on his cheek. She cried when she lifted the boy's shirt and saw the telltale bruising on his ribs. She stared murderously toward the direction of the house, where her husband waited.

I was crying now as well. "Delilah, what happened to the boy? Is he okay?"

Delilah stopped and gazed at me tenderly.

"He lives, if that's what you mean." A breeze picked up and swirled her golden hair around her face.

"Who was that boy? Do I know him?" I had to know everything now. Why would she show that to me if there was nothing I could have done about it?

Sorrow welled up in me. I could not remember feeling that sad, even when my—

"Don't you see what's happening?" My guide wrung her hands, then took my hands in hers.

I shook my head. I didn't know what she meant.

The breeze rose up again, tickling the leaves on the trees, and for the first time, through the greenery, I noticed the river, running furiously, foaming powerfully, threatening to spill over and flood the road.

"Sam, remember . . ." She paused for a moment, seemingly to get strength. She glanced over her shoulder, gazing into the water. "If you die that way, your pain comes with you. . ."

And with that, she was gone. I was left alone, by the big oak tree with the swing. Not knowing what else to do, I sat down in the swing to think for a moment.

ELIZABETH

As much as I hated to, I was forced to go to the store for supplies. Delilah didn't have any milk left, and I wasn't sure what had happened to the goat, so I needed to get some powdered milk for her. We also didn't have much left to eat at all: a few potatoes, a side of pork bacon that was mostly fat, and a little bit of beans. I didn't even have any flour to make bread with.

Billy had made some more money working for Antonio. I suspected that Antonio was a whiskey runner. All of a sudden, there seemed to be a lot more booze in town, and it wasn't like everybody suddenly got rich. It explained a lot about how Billy was able to bring home so much cash and why Antonio had moved to town. We weren't the kind of town that would attract newcomers; there just wasn't anything here. No jobs, no money, no schools, except for a small one-room schoolhouse that only taught kids to the sixth grade. If you weren't born here with family ties, you probably wouldn't like it.

As I made my way to the store, I thought about how much I loved it there. The river, fast-moving and ever changing, carved its way through the high, stone cliffs, whitewashed by thousands of years of the beating Arkansas sun. It was unspeakably beautiful, and somehow a part of me. The old mill, forever dipping its wooden fingers down into the cool spring water, had been there since my grandmother was a girl. There were caves, cool and mysterious, hidden in those cliffs, with paintings from the Cherokees, some of which were the tribe that my daddy had descended from.

In fact, the name War Eagle was from an old legend about a Cherokee brave who was devastated by the kidnapping of his one and only love, a beautiful maiden named Se-qua-dee. For days, he combed the wild mountains by the river, in search of her. According to the legend, he came upon the camp of the loggers who had taken her, and in his haste to kill her abductors and retrieve his love, he was surprised by some of the loggers that were nearby, and they killed him as well. When Se-qua-dee saw the blood of War Eagle spilled upon the rocks, she became overcome with such grief that she was said to have died from a broken heart not long after.

A lot of people, particularly people with no Indian blood, said the story was unfounded. But those of us that were Cherokee believed. Now and again, I would sleep on a blanket on the banks of the War Eagle River, and let its song calm me. Sometimes, I felt the blood of Se-qua-dee running though my veins. And sometimes, I thought I could hear the sound of her tears, her mourning never ceasing. How well I knew that sound.

EDEN

I really needed to do some laundry. I had nothing to wear to the hospital except a faded 'Mr. Mister: The Broken Wings Tour' T-shirt. I sighed and put it on, along with my faded jeans that had a torn knee. Oh well. At least they fit. Since Sam had been in the hospital, I had lost about ten pounds.

Today was Sam's birthday. How differently I had imagined the day: a huge party in the backyard, maybe a barbeque if it was warm enough. Balloons, streamers, the loud music she loved, her friends everywhere, all of our family there.

Sam seemed thinner, too. Again, the *whoosh* of the ventilator and the *beep* of the monitors was the only sound I could hear. Sam's eyes, blank and unseeing, peeked out from under her eyelids slightly. I shivered, thinking how close to dead she appeared. For a second, I imagined her in a casket instead of a bed. A cold chill overtook me and I had to leave the room.

I went out to the desk to get some coffee. I poured a large cup and drank it quickly, ignoring the burning in my throat. Mike sat at the nurses' desk, writing in Sam's chart. He saw me and smiled.

"Eden, come have a seat. I have good news about Sam."

Boy was I ready for that. I pulled up one of the maroon office chairs and sat next to him. He was wearing a navy blue shirt, red tie, and gray slacks. His blond hair was combed meticulously and he smelled of aftershave..

"Eden, we've weaned Sam down to almost nothing on the ventilator. The nurses are going to start trying to wake Sam up for short periods of time, and then gradually long periods of time. The goal is to stop sedating her. As you have seen in your patients, she might be disoriented at first, but after she is more lucid we are going to take her off the ventilator."

Tears came to my eyes. This was a turning point for Sam. If she could make it on her own, and breathe by herself, then we would have a better picture of Sam's condition.

I nodded, the tears running down my face. I took a deep breath and exhaled. Mike's blue eyes, warm and expressive, rested on mine. For a second, I caught my breath.

"I was hoping, too, that maybe I could see you later, you know, after we get Sam situated. Maybe have a quiet dinner somewhere? Does that sound okay to you?"

WAR EAGLE WOMEN | 98

"Like a date?" I blurted.

The corners of his mouth curved up into a smile and he laughed. "Yeah, Eden, like a date."

"Okay." Man, I was totally brilliant in times like those.

I saw something there, when I saw my eyes reflected in his. I saw something that looked like love.

1985

I remembered that day when I went to see Mama at the hospital, the day that Bruce came with me. Mama was lying in the hospital bed, still covered with bandages almost head to toe. Her face was trying to heal, and the bruises were in various colors of purple and yellow. She looked half dead.

"Mama?" I whispered, half afraid she would wake up and half afraid she wouldn't. Her bruised eyelids fluttered like a bird's wing and displayed her tired emerald eyes.

"Eden, you're here." She looked around, more alert than I'd anticipated. "Who brought you here?" Her eyes narrowed suspiciously.

"Bruce brought me, Mama. You know I can't drive myself." Mama was wearing a faded hospital gown, white with a blue print, and it swallowed her.

"Bruce, huh?" Mama smiled, or actually, it was more of a leer. She peered out of the room and saw him sitting in a chair waiting for me to come out. "I guess you two have been getting pretty cozy over at the Cleaver's, huh?"

My heart seemed to come up in my throat. How could Mama, who had only seen me for five seconds, perceive something that Joy was around every day and didn't?

"No, Mama," I said, shame welling up and showing in my cheeks. Then, I got angry. Very angry. "Besides, Mama, what business is it of yours?" I demanded, glaring at her.

Mama eyed me with a combination of newfound respect and irritation. "Hey, no reason to get all sassy with me! I'm kinda proud of you, kid." She glanced out the window to Bruce again. "Finally, you get some backbone. Still, he's too old for you. Plus, Joy and the kids are kind of a drag." She laughed.

It made my anger escalate to rage. "Hey, Mama, do you remember *why* I have been staying at the Cleaver's, as you put it? Remember why I'm not at my own house, in my own room? Huh?"

Mama seemed to sink down in the bed a little. She seemed confused. I never spoke to her in that way my whole life.

"Yes, Mama, let's talk about *that*. Let's talk about the fact that Julian beat you senseless, and almost killed you. Let's talk about you being so whacked on drugs and booze that you suck as a mom. You only care about yourself, never me. You're not a mother, you're a whore, Mama."

Mama glared at me, her green eyes flashing. Over in the corner of the room, her monitor started dinging. I guess my words were upsetting her and causing her heart rate to increase. *Good*, I thought to myself. *Better hers than mine*.

"So if anything happens that shouldn't, *you* are to blame, Mama," I said, tears pouring down my face. "What's going to happen to me when you die, huh? When you snort one too many hits of coke or inject one too many hits of heroin?" I demanded, leaning into her face.

She didn't know what to think. What started out as something to be amused about had turned into something uncomfortable. And Mama didn't do uncomfortable.

"Who's going to take care of me, Mama? One of your loser men that you slut around with? No, thanks. So I guess I'll just be a foster kid, won't that be great? Why did you have me, Mama? Why didn't you just abort me?" I was sobbing now, and Mama was crying, too, and avoiding my eyes. I got right in her face and repeated my question.

Mama sat up in her bed on her elbows and looked me right in the eye and said, "I tried, but it was too late."

I gasped at her bluntness. She'd tried to kill me; she'd never wanted me.

Bruce had heard me getting loud and had appeared in the room. He took me by my shoulders and escorted me out before Mama's nurse did.

I cried all the way to the truck. Bruce opened the door for me, and I somehow climbed in. I noticed in the vanity mirror that the makeup that I had so carefully applied was smeared now. The mascara had mixed with my tears, creating a raccoon effect.

Bruce didn't turn the truck down the street where we lived. Instead, we just kept driving down Highway 45. I was too upset to ask any questions. He turned off the road onto a one-lane bridge that led to the old mill. Finally, he parked his truck and we sat in front of the creek. He left the engine running and the radio playing. The sun was going down quickly, the way it did in an Arkansas winter.

"Listen, Eden," Bruce began, clearing his throat. "I didn't hear much of what your mother said, but I heard the part about you telling her off." His cigarette glowed orange in the semi-darkness.

He rolled his window down and I could hear the night sounds of the river. The storm had not missed the river. The trees were covered in ice and shone like spun sugar, a scene from a fairy tale. Chunks of ice floated in the water, but it did not stop the urgency of the river. The icy water lapped the shore and the moon was partially hidden by the thin fingers of the clouds.

I didn't say anything. My head felt like it was going to explode already, and speech seemed impossible. I wasn't sobbing any more, but still hiccupping occasionally. "Look, I don't know what you want me to say," I said angrily. "I don't need a lecture from you. You're not my dad, you know."

He exhaled a rush of breath, and ran his fingers through his hair. A bitter laugh escaped his lips, along with some smoke from his cigarette. He took one last drag and threw it out his window.

"You know, for an honor student, you're not very smart," he said, looking out the window at the remaining ember that had fallen on a river rock. It glowed for a few seconds and went dark, blending in with the night.

"What's that supposed to mean?" I demanded, fresh tears flooding my face, blending in with my mascara. "What kind of thing is that to say to somebody?"

"Do you really think of me as that old? Like somebody that's trying to be your dad?"

When he turned, I saw his face in the glow of the radio. What I saw there made me catch my breath. He was so close to me I was sure he could hear my heart beating out of my chest. His brown eyes locked on mine and I saw how much he wanted me.

Without another thought, I impulsively leaned over and kissed him. He stiffened for a second, then seemed to melt into the kiss as if he couldn't help it. Our tongues met urgently, and I felt a fire start in me that I hadn't felt before. Suddenly, he pushed me away angrily.

"What did you do that for?" he asked, clearly frazzled. His hands shook as he tried to light another cigarette. Finally, he just gave up and threw the lighter down onto the floorboard of the truck.

"I don't know," I blurted out, feeling the tears once again. "I thought—"

"No, you didn't think. That's what's wrong with you." He swallowed a couple of times as if he was having trouble thinking straight.

"Don't you like me, Bruce?" I asked, moving closer to him.

"This is all wrong," he said, shaking his head as if to clear it. "I'm married, Eden, and you're just a kid, for chrissake." He pressed himself up against the driver's side door, as if I had the plague. It made me laugh

"Do you really think I'm just a kid?" I asked, lowering my eyes like I had seen Mama do so often. I reached up and touched his face, feeling the shadow of his beard, rough and exciting on my fingers.

He shuddered. "Quit playing with me, Eden," he muttered, breathless and angry at the same time.

"I'm not playing with you, Bruce," I said, running my fingers around the collar of his shirt. He stiffened again and pushed my fingers away. "If you really didn't want me, why did you come here, if not to be alone with me?"

"Don't push it," he warned, "you don't want to play a grown-up game." He reached for his keys to start the truck.

I grabbed the keys, and threw them out his window.

"What the hell?" Bruce yelled, furious, but when he saw the grin on my face, he couldn't help laughing. "Seriously, Eden, you need to grow up."

I kept my eyes on him as I took off my jean jacket.

"What are you doing? How can you possibly be hot?" he asked stupidly.

I peeled off my blouse, and before Bruce could say anything, I had unbuttoned my bra and slipped it off my arm expertly.

Bruce was breathing heavily, and looked mad as hell.

"So, do you think I still need to grow up now?" I scooted over toward him. I put my fingers around his neck and pressed my lips onto his, my bare breasts against him. I was acting just like Mama, and I knew it. I'd learned her tricks well.

He shuddered.

"Don't you want to touch me, Bruce?" I asked, kissing his neck, and unbuttoning his shirt as I did.

He moaned, and any reserve left in him disappeared then. In a minute, his lips and hands were all over me.

I held his head there as he nuzzled me, his tongue in the valley between my breasts, his hand up my skirt. In a minute, I was totally naked in front of him, and even though it was dark, the moon illuminated my skin like a spotlight.

"God, you're beautiful…you really are like the Garden of Eden." He stared at me in the moonlight. In the winter chill, our hunger for each other made us sweat.

Somehow, in the small space of the truck, Bruce found his way inside me. When my legs wrapped around him, and a second of excruciating pain came and went, I did not make a peep. I focused instead on the sound of the river rushing by.

EMILY

I'm not sure what was going on with Spencer. He was up and down. One day he called me back right away, and the next he didn't call me for a week. I felt hurt and a little desperate, so I put on my cutest outfit, spent extra time doing my hair, and I waited for him by his locker before second block. He saw me standing there, and I saw him roll his eyes. He came over to the locker, looking mad.

"Emily, what are you doing?" he asked, annoyed, as he practically shouldered his way in and opened the locker.

I pretended not to notice. "Nothing," I said, putting on another layer of lip-gloss. "I'm just wondering if you want to come over today."

At that, he closed his eyes in irritation, and slammed his locker. "I don't think so, Emily," he said, coldly gazing past me.

"What's going on with you? I never see you anymore." I asked him.

He looked embarrassed when people walked by and heard our conversation. "Shhh, can't we talk about this later?" he asked, checking his messages on his iPhone.

That really annoyed me. "No, I want to talk now. Why have you been acting so weird? Why do you hardly call me anymore?"

"Look, Emily, it's not like we're married. Maybe we should break up if you are planning to turn into a crazy stalker chick."

I felt the heat flush across my face, and an unreasonable rage flowed through me.

"Break up? You want to break up with me?" I shrieked, in a voice that was louder than I'd intended.

I saw a slow grin spread across his lips, and I scanned across the room to where his eyes were focused. He was leering at Jessica Myers, who'd been my best friend in junior high. And who was totally dressed like a slut.

ELIZABETH

The town had tried to dress up the store and church with Christmas decorations in a lame attempt to bring festivity to War Eagle. It didn't do much for me except make me remember Mama and how she'd tried to make Christmas special for us, even when Daddy drank away the Christmas money. All it made me think of was that I hoped this year would hurry and be over. I had high hopes for 1941.

I was almost at the store when I saw Henry Portland on the opposite side of the road. He waved… Henry was Isabelle's son and was a year older than I was in school. He was tall and reddish-blond and pale-skinned. He had a cleft in his chin that I always found attractive.

"Hi, Elizabeth," he called, grinning ear-to-ear.

I thought he had grown taller since the last time I had seen him. He was slender, but not skinny. Henry, for as long as I had known him, had always wanted to go to school to be a preacher. That was pretty much enough for me to not take him seriously.

"Hi, Henry. How are you?"

He fell into step next to me. He was holding a basket of

eggs. "Oh, the same. I'm taking these eggs to Mr. Ferrell to see if he will buy them from me."

Oh, thank goodness. A way out! "Henry, I wonder if you would do me a favor?" I asked, trying to be as charming as I could.

"For you, Elizabeth? Anything," he replied, a flirty grin played around his lips.

I was taken aback for a moment. I had never seen that side of him.

"Well, I have some money here, and I needed a few things, but—" I stopped short, not knowing how to proceed. How could I explain without telling too much?

"Ah, I think I understand." Henry smiled. "You don't want to go in the store because your dad owes money?" He paused expectantly.

"How . . . how did you know that?"

"Silly, Elizabeth. I think you forgot for a minute where you live at. This is War Eagle. Everybody knows everything about everybody here." *Not everything,* I thought silently to myself. I suspected everyone had a few dark secrets, but probably none as dark as mine. My cheeks flushed with shame.

"You know, never mind," I said, and started marching back to the cabin, my eyes stinging with tears.

Henry had to nearly run to catch up with me. "I'm sorry, Elizabeth," he said breathlessly. "Please forgive me. I would never hurt your feelings on purpose. Let me help you."

I stopped for a moment. I really did need the supplies, and I really did not need to see Mr. Ferrell.

"Besides, don't you know there's a depression on?" He smiled, his face kind and reassuring. "Everybody owes Mr. Ferrell something."

"Well, okay," I said, giving him my list and the cash I had gotten from Billy. "Thanks," I added, smiling back at him. I decided to sit on one of the stumps of an abandoned oak tree and wait for him to come back.

That's when I saw Daddy, coming down the street with Carolyn and her daughter, Susan. Susan was skipping in the middle of the two of them, holding hands with them.

I felt my heart in my throat to see them that way. What nerve Daddy had to be strolling down town, all dressed up in a suit and boldly parading his "other" family around. I hid behind the tree so he couldn't see me.

From there I watched Daddy go into the store, Susan happily tagging along and Carolyn following close behind. What a perfect picture they made. Daddy, his new wife, and his pretty little look-alike daughter.

Not like me. I was a too cruel reminder of the wife that had died, that he had, in my eyes at least, helped kill. I wondered how long it would be until he destroyed Carolyn as well.

I also wondered how Daddy could go in that store knowing he owed Mr. Ferrell money. Was he ready to pay up? Could I stop being afraid of a visit from him?

A few minutes later, Henry came out, holding my supplies. He searched around for me for a minute, and when he saw me, his face was all smiles. He came over and said, "Hey, do you need a hand with these? I could carry them to your house for you, if you like."

I thanked him. We went back to the cabin and I couldn't resist asking about Daddy. "So, did you talk to my father in the store?" I asked, trying to act like I didn't really care.

"No, he didn't really notice me. But I do think there's something you should know." Henry bit his lip.

I felt nervous. This couldn't be good news.

"What? Did he not pay his bill?" I had really hoped that was why he felt all right about going in there. I mean, Mr. Ferrell was not going to sell him anything unless he did. At least not on credit. And Daddy always bought everything on credit.

"No, he paid it," Henry said, avoiding my eyes.

"What then? Just tell me," I demanded.

"Elizabeth, he had to pay it or Mr. Ferrell wouldn't let him place his order." He looked at me. "Elizabeth, your dad was buying a wedding ring."

ELIZABETH

Eden just called to tell me they had taken Sam off the ventilator. I had to get over there and see her. It was about an hour drive to Fayetteville in that kind of traffic. Fayetteville was kind of big city compared to War Eagle, but not to a lot of other places.

The drive gave me some time to think about things. I thought about Sam, Eden, Emily, and my mother. I also remembered Delilah and Diane. So much pain, so many years ago.

Back then, I just didn't know what to say or do about Daddy getting married. It was good in a way, I guessed, because that meant at least theoretically he was going to have to keep his nose clean. He had a wife now, and a daughter, and he didn't want to screw things up. A new beginning. And Billy and I were left holding what remained of the old life, a life he'd rather forget.

Of course Billy, Delilah, Jacob and I were not exactly invited to the wedding. But what was Daddy going to do about us? He couldn't just pretend like we didn't exist. And what kind of woman would Carolyn be if she let him? Didn't she know, at least on some basic level, that how he treated us would one day be the way he treated Susan?

I was pinning laundry on the clothesline when I saw her drive up, with Daddy in the car with her. I didn't exactly greet her with open arms, and I didn't think she was used to being glared at the way I was glaring at her.

"Elizabeth, do you have a minute?" she asked awkwardly.

I finished hanging the last of the clothes and nodded. We went to sit on the porch. I didn't offer her anything to drink.

In my mind, she was partially responsible for Mama's death, and I wasn't about to roll out the red carpet for a killer.

"I guess you have heard the news by now that your dad and I are getting married."

I noticed the ring on her left hand, a simple solitaire that shone in the sun.

"Yeah, I think I heard something about it," I replied.

"Elizabeth, I know how you feel about your dad, and I can guess how you feel about me. But I want you to know I want to take care of you all. I came to ask you to move in with me and your daddy."

"What?" I asked, dumbfounded. That was the last thing I'd expected. "Look, that's not really necessary. Billy is eighteen now, and so he's kind of acting like our guardian." I wasn't sure how legal that arrangement was, but since Daddy didn't really give a crap about us, and had never challenged it or tried to take care of us, it just had never came up.

"I thought you might say that." Carolyn smiled.

In different circumstances, I might have liked her, but I couldn't let my guard down. In doing so, I would be dishonoring Mama's memory.

"Look, I'm not here to make your life more difficult," Carolyn explained. "And I don't want to make an enemy of you. I'd like to one day be your friend."

At this I laughed, a hostile sound from a bitter well.

"I appreciate your offer of friendship," I answered sarcastically.

"I don't think you understand what I'm getting at," she protested angrily.

"No, I really don't. Unless you are planning on giving us money to eat on. Your fiancé doesn't much care if we eat or not."

"I can't afford to support another household, and that's not what the plan was, anyway," Carolyn retorted, her blue eyes flashing angrily.

"What do you want from me, Carolyn?" I demanded. "You wanted my Daddy, and you got him, God help you. I hope you can hold him."

Her smile that she had been forcing completely faded.

"You know, he was horrible to my mother," I continued. "And I don't just mean the cheating, although there was plenty of that."

Carolyn began to look around uneasily.

"He used to beat her. Once he almost killed her with one of the beatings. That was the day he raped her and Delilah was conceived." Carolyn began growing pale, and I knew I should probably stop, but I was getting a perverse pleasure from making her uncomfortable.

"Yeah, that was really a special moment in the Graham household," I said, crossing my arms. "I tried to leave, to go get help, but he wouldn't let me." I paused for a breath. "He forced me to watch while he raped her. And then he threatened to do the same thing to me. Did you know that, Carolyn? I mean, I'm pretty sure by now you know he is a drunk, and hardly ever can hold a job. I suspect you may have already noticed his wandering eye, but I'm willing to bet you didn't know most of what I just told you."

"Stop it! You are a horrible child, just like your daddy told me. He knew you would be this way, but I didn't believe him."

"Well, that's a good place to start, the not believing him, I mean."

Carolyn sighed and rubbed her forehead like she was getting a headache. "Look, the main thing I wanted to tell you is this: You don't have to come and live with your father and me, but I will have to take Delilah and Jacob. They are too young to stay here with you like this. You are not their mother."

"I'm the closest thing they have to a mother! You can't take them away from me," I said, trying to be brave but knowing I had no legal ground to stand on. "Do you even really want them?"

"They are young enough, I think they will grow to love me and accept me as their mama."

"You can't have them."

"Elizabeth, you can give them to me now, or I can go get the sheriff. I was hoping we could be civil like and skip all that, but I can do it that way if I have to. Besides, Elizabeth, don't you want to go back to school? I mean, you don't really like all this housewife stuff, do you? You are a bit young to give yourself up to this kind of life."

She had me there. I was too young to give everything up. But everything in me resisted letting this woman have Mama's babies. Then again, what choice did I have?

Jacob had woken up from his nap and came out in the living room rubbing his eyes. His hair was sticking up in all directions. Carolyn smiled at him, and kneeled down to his level to speak to him.

"Hi, Jacob, how are you?" she asked kindly.

"Good," Jacob answered.

I went to him and put my arm around him and gave him a kiss. He still smelled like sleep and sunshine. He was really cute that morning, and it was tearing me apart. The tears were pooling in the corners of my eyes and I didn't know how long I could keep them at bay.

I glimpsed out the window and saw Daddy sitting in the car. *What a coward,* I thought to myself. *It just shows how little he wanted us. He was just going along with it because she wanted the little ones for her own.*

Jacob saw Daddy outside and ran out to him. In spite of himself, Daddy smiled. And when Carolyn brought Delilah to him, he began to cry. A few moments later, he stepped up to the porch.

I hardly recognized him. He had his hair cut short, and

was wearing a clean and pressed white shirt and new brown trousers. He was clearly sober.

"Elizabeth," he began, running his fingers through his dark hair, "I know you hate me, and I can understand. But I want you to know, I've changed. I don't drink anymore, and I know the pain I caused you all. I wish you would reconsider and come live with us."

Neither of us spoke. The only sounds were that of a mockingbird calling its mate, and the ever-present roll of the river.

"I don't want to, Daddy. I'm happy here. Isn't it enough that you are taking the babies from me? I've become their mama, you know."

"I know, and I'm sorry fer that. I won't make you come live with me, but I will take care of you from now on. You have to believe that." His green Irish eyes bored into mine.

"No, Daddy, I don't," I said quietly, managing not to cry.

Daddy went into the house, letting the old screen door slam behind him. Through the screen, I watched as he went to the kitchen and left a wad of bills on the table before turning to me.

"You are old enough to be on your own now, if you want. There's nothing I can do about that."

And with that, he took the babies, and they were gone. Bitterness filled my throat and hatred pumped through my veins. It was easier than hurting. I sat on the porch and watched them until I couldn't see them anymore.

ELIZABETH
The day that Daddy and Carolyn came to take the babies away was one of the darkest in my life. Billy and I made do, going through the motions of everyday living, but my heartfelt hollowed out and numb from too much pain, and too much loss. Billy tried to talk me into going back to school, but

I just couldn't make myself. Why should I, when everyone I loved went away? Why should I try to make something of myself, when everything, and everyone I loved, except for Billy, it seemed, went away or was somehow ripped away from me when I least expected it.

With the babies gone, there was hardly anything to do around the house. Billy was gone most of the day, running errands for Antonio, and if it was just me, alone, I didn't stay around the house anyway. The minute Billy left, I found myself called down to the river.

The water that time of year, late winter, was icy and dark, the color of my depression. Some leftover snow from a few weeks ago clung stubbornly to some of the brush that grew along the river. I sat on the rocky banks for a long time, just thinking about Delilah and Jacob and Mama. I would rerun those days over and over in my mind again, remembering Mama's expression when she saw the baby die, and her eyes when Daddy had hurt her so bad. I would remember how Jacob's hair smelled when he first woke up in the morning and how Delilah had smiled at me when I sung to her. I tried to think about how I might have been able to change that or how we might be back together again. If only Daddy hadn't met Carolyn, maybe Mama might still be alive. How if I had managed to be a better mother to Delilah instead of just an older sister, she might still be with me instead of living with Daddy and Carolyn. I wondered if Carolyn loved Delilah like I did. Of course she didn't. There was no way to duplicate the way I felt about those babies. I had always loved them, but after Mama died, the love I felt had changed into so much more than just sisterly love. I really did feel like their mama sometimes.

After Daddy had taken the babies to live with him, I found myself going to the river almost every morning. The woods were quiet and deserted, and the chill of the morning air made my breath visible. A fog hovered ghostlike over the river, and bits of ice floated in the dark water, giving them the appearance of hardened sugar on sheets of licorice. The leafless blackened trees reached out their thin arms to scratch the surface of the steel gray sky. It was going to snow again soon. I could feel it; I could smell it.

I was attempting to read a book of poetry by Emily Dickenson. The melancholy cadence of her words spoke to me. The river calmed me, and, as always, centered me. The sounds of the gently lapping water seemed to match my pulse. In some ways, the river had become my adoptive mother. She was constant, always there, ready to listen to me when I was upset, ranting and raving at the injustices that were part of my world.

I heard a twig snap in the far woods, but thought nothing of it at first. Even in the dead of winter, the creatures of the woods were still occasionally active. Maybe it was a deer, coming to drink of the frozen water.

I had just decided to ignore the sound when I heard it again. It startled me, making my breath catch in my chest. I felt my heart hammering, my pulse quickening. "Who's there?" I called, the echo of my voice bouncing back to me from the cliffs, white as bone.

"It's just me," I heard a low, gentle voice call.

"Who's me?" I asked, searching the woods but seeing no one. Just then, I saw a flame of reddish blond hair against the snow. Henry, carrying a fishing pole and some tackle. I felt so relieved.

"Did I scare you?" he asked, setting down his pole. "I didn't mean to." He stretched out his arms. "I guess you found my secret fishing spot. So much for secrets." He grinned at me.

Shading my eyes with my hand, I had to look up quite a ways to see him. His eyes, a warm chocolate brown, were friendly and kind. There were a few freckles, the color of light cinnamon, sprinkled across the bridge of his nose. His chin was dimpled, and it looked like he hadn't shaved this morning. Some rebel sprinkle of reddish-brown stubble peeked through his cheeks and chin. He was bundled up in a heavy winter coat and wisps of his blond hair poked out the edges of his warm woolen cap. His heavy fisherman's boots made deep footprints in the snow.

"Well, as I live and breathe, it's Henry Portland," I exclaimed, using my best southern belle impression.

He chuckled, a hearty low laugh, that surprisingly sounded just a little sexy. "What the heck is Isabelle feeding you over there? You've gotten huge!"

It was true. Henry had always been tall, at least taller than most of the boys in class, but over the school year he had really bulked up. It was apparent even in his winter gear that he had changed from a skinny beanpole kid to quite a handsome hulk sorts overnight. Of course it wasn't really overnight. It had just been a few months since I'd run into him at the store. I stood up to greet him and realized with a start that I only came up to his chin. He saw my expression and grinned again. His teeth were perfect, straight and white, and the combination of the teeth, hair, and bulk of him took me by surprise. He had turned from an ugly duckling into a swan.

"Oh!" I breathed, the smell of his aftershave dizzying me for a second. I blushed a little at my unintentional outburst. To his credit, Henry pretended not to notice. "How's the family?" I asked, trying to change the subject, still hoping he hadn't noticed how his appearance had thrown me off guard.

"Oh, they're fine, just fine." He began baiting his pole. "Mama's been sewing a lot for folks, can't seem to keep up with all the work people have been giving her. Oh, and did you hear that my Uncle Rick joined the Navy?"

I had briefly met Rick a few times, at church socials and the like, and he seemed like a nice guy. A lot wilder than Henry though.

"Really? Why?" I blurted out without thinking. I had always thought that boys joining the Navy was a foolish thing to do, especially in wartime. The winter of 1940 had not yet brought the United States into another war, but things seemed to be heating up all over the world, and though most people in War Eagle felt like America should stay out of the conflict, I wondered how long it would be before we had no choice but to get involved. "Does he plan to take on Hitler himself?" I joked, and Henry laughed too.

"Sounds like him, doesn't it? Well, he feels it's his duty. I can understand why. What are you doing out here, anyway, Elizabeth?"

"Oh, just reading, and thinking," I mumbled, wondering how in the world Henry Portland of all people could make me feel so out of sorts. For Pete's sake, I had known him since we were in diapers, our mothers being best friends and all. "I guess I *am* a little cold," I admitted. Now that he mentioned it, I was more than a little cold. My thin woolen jacket I had thrown on as I was leaving the cabin seemed to be made of Swiss cheese. I felt the chilly mountain air on my skin even under the coat. Goose bumps rose up on my arms.

Henry propped his pole up between two heavy sandstone rocks. "Here, why don't you take my coat? I wore layers underneath, so I'll be fine," he suggested.

I started to protest, but before I could, he shrugged his coat off and put it around my shoulders. It was warm and smelled like him. He was wearing a long sleeved flannel shirt, but even through the flannel, I was able to appreciate the subtle tones of his biceps.

"Pretty silly of you to come out here without a warm coat, Elizabeth," he scolded in a teasing tone.

Henry was always teasing and playing. I don't think I ever saw him serious a day in his life. His eyes always seemed to have a sparkle in them and I always felt comfortable around him, unlike Antonio, who seemed to take my breath away just with his very presence. Speaking of Antonio, I had not seen him in a few weeks. I wasn't sure what that was about. I mean, he told me he wanted to court me, then nothing.

"What are you reading?" Henry asked, his eyes on the river, not the book.

"Oh, just some poetry. Emily Dickinson," I answered, and gathered his coat around me. It was huge, and the arms extended long past my fingers. When he wasn't looking, I breathed deep into the collar. It smelled so good.

"Ha, figures," he teased, flashing those perfect teeth. "You always had your nose in a book. No wonder Mrs. Lang liked you so much. Teacher's pet." He smiled.

"Well, you might have been her pet if you hadn't been skipping school so much to go fishing," I said, grinning myself. Henry could always make me grin.

"Yeah, maybe," he agreed. "But I was never into books like you were. Except one, of course."

I knew what he meant. He was talking about the Bible. Henry was always reading the Bible, talking about the Bible, deliberating on the meaning of the scriptures. It bored me to tears.

"Yeah, I know," I responded, much more dryly than I meant to. His eyes blinked at the tone of my voice. "Sorry," I said quickly. I wasn't trying to hurt his feelings. He was nothing if not kind to me.

"That's okay," he said and walked back to his fishing pole picking it up from the rocks.

The sky had turned a leaden gray, and the breeze had picked up the slightest bit, blowing across the black waters.

"Hey, I think I got one!" he said gleefully, his cheeks flushed in excitement. For a minute, he looked like a little boy. Skillfully he reeled it in, a huge trout, silver and beautiful in the sun.

"Looks like we got lunch!" he said, his grin shining brighter than the sun.

We made a fire and he cooked the fish. We sat for hours, talking about everything. There wasn't much I hid from him. He knew most of it anyway. But there were some secrets even he didn't know.

"So, you didn't want to go live with your daddy and his new wife?" he asked, adding a log to the fire.

"Not especially. She's not my favorite person. Billy and I do okay on our own." The colors of the fire were beautiful, amber and orange and sapphire at the bottom. I felt the weight of sentiments unsaid.

"What's bothering you, Henry? You seem like you want to say something." I waited, and the only sound I could hear was my breathing and the lapping of the water.

"I don't like Billy hanging around with that Italian guy," he finally blurted out. I could tell he was uncomfortable to say it. "And I don't really like *you* hanging out with him, either," he finished, arms crossed.

"Oh, really," I said, feeling a little angry. "Do you really think it's godly to be prejudiced about him because he's Italian?" I demanded. "What do you know about him anyway?"

"Look, Elizabeth," Henry said, his cheeks flushed with anger, "I think it's a bit harsh of you to label me prejudiced. I called him Italian because I can't pronounce his name."

I giggled at that, and his jaw relaxed the slightest bit. "Antonio Bettino," I said. "His name is not important. What is important," Henry said, moving closer to me on the rock I was sitting on, so close I could smell his aftershave again, "is that he is not a good man, and I'm afraid you and Billy are going to get hurt associating yourselves with him. You know he is a whiskey runner, right, Elizabeth?"

I lowered my gaze. "I've heard something about it. It's not hurting anyone! Are you so judgmental that the issue of a little illegal booze is going to bother you? He's been paying Billy good money to help him. That's how we have been able to feed ourselves. What do you know about being hungry, Henry? You have the perfect parents, the perfect life!" I started to feel the tears come to my eyes, and was fighting my hardest to keep them from flowing. I did not want to start bawling in front of Henry. How pathetic would that be?

I could tell my tears bothered him, he had such a big heart and all. He reached over and took my hand in his. His palm was warm and a bit callused from all the farm work he was used to doing.

"Actually, Elizabeth, it's hurting a lot of people. Bettino don't brew the stuff, but he pays some of the mountain men like Joshua O'Reilly to do it. There's no regulations, so they can put whatever they want in it. Some of the older kids have been buying it and ending up in the hospital. You know Charlie Reynolds and Sam Jones? They were really sick after drinking some of that mash. Not only that, but crime has been increasing around the town, because a lot of these old mountain men don't know how to behave when they get a hold of that stuff. It's a bad deal, Elizabeth." I could see the sincerity in Henry's eyes. "These people that Bettino runs around with are hard men. They will shoot you as well as look at you. You don't want to be involved with a man like that, Elizabeth."

"Then who should I be involved with, Henry?" I flirted a little, feeling the warmth of his arm even through the coat that was draped around my shoulders.

He paused only a second, then answered me by leaning in toward me and ever so gently tucked a lock of my hair behind my ear, then touched his lips to each of my eyelids. I felt my breath catch and confusion cloud my mind. His lips touched mine, soft as a feather, and he rested his forehead on mine for a moment.

"Choose me, Elizabeth," he murmured, his lips warm on my forehead, my cheeks, my lips. His kiss was light at first, then demanding, and I lost my breath for a moment. The scent of him invaded my nostrils. He smelled of aftershave and pine, and the river. His fingertips touched my hair, then my neck, then the small of my back as he pressed me to him. I knew I needed to push him away, at least for propriety's sake but I couldn't. I started kissing him back, and before I knew it, he moved his lips away. We were both a bit breathless.

"Well, what do you think of that?" He laughed, and so did I.

We stood there for a moment, with only the sounds of our ragged breathing and the waves licking the shore.

After that, I found myself coming to the river every morning. I was aware on some level it was to see Henry, but I didn't dwell on it. Henry, I knew, was doing his morning chores at a furious rate in order to find the time to come see me. When he did come, we would sit for an hour or so on our rock, and hold hands and talked. I didn't know where it was going but I knew that Henry wanted to be a preacher, and I was no preacher's wife.

I believed in God, of course. Anyone living on the banks of the War Eagle River would believe in God. The beauty of the river shouted the testimony of being created by a higher being. But I had to wonder, if God was real, how could He allow the things that happened in my family? How could He allow what happened to my mother, dead so young? How could He allow my father to start over with his new family like nothing ever happened, as if the wife of his youth wasn't rotting in a crude pine coffin? It didn't seem fair. And if God wasn't fair, then who was?

One morning after I had my morning visit with Henry, I made my way back to the cabin. It was springtime in the mountains, and flowers were blooming everywhere. Mama's roses especially were budding overnight. I continued up the road from the river and my breath caught. Antonio was sitting on the porch waiting for me. My heart leapt in my throat as I tried to act happy to see him. I was happy on some level. Antonio's refined good looks still got to me, but there was fear there as well.

"Elizabeth!" He stood.

That day was no exception. He looked wonderful as always. White shirt, starched and buttoned all the way to the top, charcoal gray slacks and dark leather boots. He wore a dark gray fedora hat as well, and it sat on his ebony curls with attitude. He looked wonderful, dangerous, and sexy. I tried to read his expression to see if he knew anything, but he was too smooth to give away his feelings.

I stepped up on the porch and within a second, he took me in his arms and began kissing me until I couldn't think. He smelled of expensive cologne. Finally, I pushed him away.

His eyes narrowed suspiciously. "What's wrong, Elizabeth?" he asked quietly, removing his hat and tossing it on the old chair. "Are you not happy to see me?" His perfectly groomed moustache had felt good on my skin, and when it brushed the place where my neck and collarbone met, it literally took my breath away.

"Of course I'm glad to see you, Antonio," I said, and it wasn't a lie. How could any woman resist him? He was the representation of pure sex. I was not sophisticated enough to defend myself around him. He was smarter, more worldly.

"I'm sorry I have not been around for a while. I was called away for business," he explained, his brown eyes boring into mine.

"Oh," I said simply, sitting down in the chair next to his. "I wondered what happened to you."

"I got back as soon as I could," he said sincerely, reaching over for my hand.

I folded my hands in my lap. He laughed at me. "Are you upset with me, *Cara?*"

I looked at him quizzically and he laughed.

"Oh, I'm sorry, *Cara* means"—I could tell he was searching through his personal Italian-English dictionary—"Sweetheart, Darling," he said, with a heavy accent. I knew he probably called ever girl he ever met *Cara*. It was part of his smoothness. I crossed my arms.

"And, just so you know"—he leaned over and picked up his hat from the chair—"I don't call everyone *Cara*." Then he walked down the steps and left.

ELIZABETH

I went to the river again the next morning. I guessed I was hoping to see Henry again, as usual. I didn't think he really spent that much time fishing before, but all of a sudden he'd turned into some kind of fishing fool. I was so conflicted about Henry. On the one hand, I felt kind of fuzzy about him. When I was with him, he seemed like the one I should be with, but when I was with Antonio, however briefly, it seemed the opposite. I was such a silly girl. I couldn't honestly see myself marrying Henry though, because of the God issue. It was too weird.

But what really bothered me about Henry was he had not really made his intentions clear. That was confusing as well. He never formally asked me to be his girl or anything like that. He just showed up all the time at the river, every day at 7:30.

I asked the river, but she didn't answer.

I had to go into town that day. We had almost nothing to eat at the house. Daddy wasn't really trying at all to bring us anything anymore, and the vegetables and fruits that I'd helped Mama can were almost gone. The situation was getting a little desperate.

Billy had given me some money, a fairly large wad, and I didn't really ask any questions. I knew it was wrong, and probably gained in an unlawful manner. Whenever I felt guilty about where it came from, I reminded myself that this was my father's fault for not taking care of us. We did what we had to do. Daddy could carry the sin of our indiscretions.

When I came into the middle of town, I could hardly make my way through the crowd.. It seemed that everybody from town was there. I saw Isabelle and her kids standing by the store. Isabelle was talking to some of the other town folks, including my old teacher, Mrs. Lang. Both women had been crying. I ran over to ask them what was happening, but was almost knocked over by a crowd of boys including some from school that were all hanging out of the back of Mr. O'Neill's truck. They slowed down to let me cross, and when I asked them, "Where are y'all off to in such a hurry?"

Joshua O'Reilly leaned out the window and shouted, "The Japanese bombed Pearl Harbor! They say that they might be back to bomb California, too. We're goin' to join the Army!"

I stood there dumbfounded. "What? When did this happen?" But the boys were too busy speeding down the dirt road that led down the center of town to go enlist.

We stood there for a while, just watching the mixed reactions of the people in the street. Old men were standing out in the dirt street, reminiscing about their glory days of the Great War and how it was certain that the United States would be forced to be involved in this present conflict. The women were in tears, some for people they knew, and some for the tears that were going to be shed in the future. The fear was that the draft would be started up soon. Everybody was thinking about their own sons and husbands and wondering who would be the first. Mostly, everyone was enraged at the Japanese. Many wanted any people with even a drop of Japanese blood out of the country immediately. And a lot of people were convinced that, now that the Japanese had wiped out Pearl Harbor, they would move to a closer target inland. People were scared.

"I'm worried about Rick. I called my sister but she hasn't heard anything yet. They don't have a list of the dead yet," Isabelle said quietly, her voice flat and without emotion. Suddenly, as if saying the words made a fictional event real, she began to sob, wrenching cries that chilled me to the bone.

"Isabelle!" I said, not knowing what to do. I put my arm around her and helped her back to her house. David was waiting for us, and ran out to meet us. He took Isabelle in his arms and physically carried her up the steps and into their house. Isabelle looked like a child in his arms. She leaned on him, spent and broken. He took her and put her to bed.

I cried too, seeing them. That was what I wanted. Not necessarily someone to take care of me, but that kind of love. I wanted someone to hold on to, like Isabelle held on to David.

I stayed for a while and cooked dinner for the family, although it wasn't really necessary. Word had spread fast about Rick, and people responded the only way they knew how: food. Everybody knew Rick and liked him. More than that, they all knew Isabelle and loved her. Isabelle didn't have any family close by, and it was doubtful that they would have the money to send her to her sister's house in St. Louis where the funeral would be held.

While I was washing dishes, and Henry was drying, David yelled out, "Hey, President Roosevelt's giving a speech!" We dropped everything to go listen. Finally, about 9:00, I decided to go home and check on Billy. I had not seen him since this morning. When I went back to the cabin, Billy was there.

"Did you hear? About Rick, I mean?" I asked.

He nodded.

"Isabelle is devastated, Henry and David, too."

"Elizabeth, I-I have something to tell you," he began, crunching his knuckles. He often did that when he was worried or stressed.

It made my stomach clench in a knot to see him do that. "What is it?" I asked, my eyes following his.

"Elizabeth, I have to get out of here," he said, his eyes looking somewhere far away. "I don't want to stay here anymore. Nobody expects anything from me, except to turn out like Daddy. The girls in town, they laugh at me, like I ain't good enough for them." He balled up his fists. "I can't get work no more, unless it's from Antonio, and I don't want to do that anymore. I've seen too much." His brow furrowed.

"Well, okay," I answered, confused. "I don't know where we can go with no money, or no relatives to help us. Nobody cares about us, Billy, you know that." I looked at my feet. When I raised my eyes back to Billy, I was taken aback by the steely hard look in his eye. It made me shudder involuntarily. He looked just like Daddy when he did that.

"Look, this is my fault," I said, reaching out to take his hand in mine. "I've been sitting around here, moping for Mama and the babies, and leaving everything for you to take care of. That wasn't fair of me."

He laughed bitterly then. "Elizabeth, this is not your fault. This is Daddy's fault for leaving us here to fend for ourselves. You're just a kid. I'm supposed to take care of you, but I can't do it anymore, I just can't."

"I'm not six years old, Billy," I said, lifting my chin defiantly. "You don't have to take care of anyone. I can help earn money. We don't need much."

"Elizabeth, I joined the Army," he blurted out.

I gasped in disbelief. "What? Why?" I heard the wind outside start to howl a sad song.

"Because I want to get out of here, like I said. I don't want to be in his town, where everyone knows me as the town drunk's boy. Where the only work I can get is directly responsible for destroying the lives of others." He ran his fingers through his hair.

"The Army? Are you crazy?" I demanded.

"No, I'm not crazy. I leave Thursday," he said quietly. "I'm just gonna be drafted anyway."

"Thursday! Oh God." I fell back onto the couch, and started crying.

"Elizabeth, shhhh. Don't cry." Billy put his arm around me. "It will be better, you'll see. Things will look up for us if I have a real job. I can send you money! We won't be scrounging around anymore."

"Ha! You call that a real job? Getting your behind shot off?" I screeched at him.

"Yeah, that might happen, but I'll be careful. Elizabeth, America is at war. We can't ignore it anymore. You don't want me to be a coward, do you?"

I saw my own green eyes looking back at me. "Well, what am I supposed to do? Do I stay here alone?" I suddenly thought of the empty cabin, and how lonely that would be. "No, Elizabeth. I don't think that's safe." Billy said.

"Well, I'm not going to Daddy. That's not going to happen."

"I know, I wasn't expecting that either. I think you should go stay with Isabelle."

"No."

"Why, Elizabeth? Don't you like Isabelle anymore?" He raised a brow at me quizzically.

"No, it's not that. I just don't want to have anybody bossing me around. I'm used to being on my own, or just the two of us. I'm seventeen now. There are women on this mountain that already have a couple of kids by now. You go, Billy. I'll be fine."

ELIZABETH

I never knew if Billy talked to him or not, because he left shortly after for basic training. All I knew was, after that, that I couldn't get rid of Henry. In the mornings when he went fishing, I would meet him down the riverbank.

Maybe it wasn't the most romantic thing in the world but I thought it was really cute when he bought me my own river waders. Every day he would give me a new fishing lesson. Surprisingly, I enjoyed it. Then at night he would come over to the cabin and I would read my poetry. I was also working on a book, my first novel. A historical set in the time of the explorers about an Indian maiden, loosely based on my grandmother, my dad's mom. Henry told me it was good, but I knew he was just prejudiced. I could write anything and he said it was brilliant. I could write a grocery list and he would call it poetry.

One day I went down to the river to meet Henry. I had packed a lunch of fried chicken, potato salad, apple pie, and iced tea. The harsh winter, like always, had melted into spring and flowers were blooming all over the riverbank. The river changed from black to brown, and the trees went from bare to leafy green once again. The animals were coming out from their winter rest hungry and thirsty as they made their way to the river. I was reading *Walden* while I waited for Henry. I couldn't wait to read a passage to him that I found fascinating.

I was deep into the text and almost didn't notice the sound of a twig snapping behind me and turned around to smile at Henry but it wasn't him.

"Daddy?" I asked in disbelief.

The man in front of me barely resembled my father and he was obviously very upset. His clothes were dirty and wrinkled and when he staggered closer to me I could smell the whiskey on his breath. His unshaven cheeks were flushed from the drink.

"What you doing? What's wrong with you?" I sputtered, feeling like something wasn't right. Since he'd been with Carolyn, rumor had it he didn't drink any more. But that day, he'd had plenty to drink. He came toward me, his gait unsteady, his finger pointed at me.

"You. You're what's wrong. You did this," he slurred, barely able to stand.

"I-I don't know what you mean," I stuttered, backing away from him.

He stopped pursuing me for a moment, and reached into his jacket for his bottle of whiskey which was nearly gone. He took a long drink, finishing it off. Then he threw the bottle as hard as he could into the river. He shook his head as if to clarify his vision, and then began yelling at me again.

"Carolyn, she . . . threw me out. She said I was with another woman."

"Well, were you?" I asked, biding my time, wondering where Henry was.

Daddy raked his fingers through his hair, and for a second I felt sorry for him. But when his eyes met mine, I saw the dark glimmer of his rage. A slow grin spread across his lips.

"So what if I was?" He sneered. "She was freezing me out. I don't have to take that. I got plenty of other offers. Women want me all the time. I ain't gonna play those games with any woman. I didn't play 'em with your Mama, and I sure ain't gonna play them with the likes of Carolyn. She sleeps around, too, you know."

"Daddy, what does this have to do with me? I don't tell Carolyn what to do, and nobody can tell Mama what to do, can they?"

All of a sudden, he lunged at me, his hand around my throat squeezing and squeezing. I tried to scream but of course I couldn't.

"She said you told her that I killed your mother. She said you told her that I beat your mother and made her crazy."

His eyes darkened with rage, and the sky around me was blackening at the edges. All I could hear was the sound of the river rushing by as I fell back on the rocks. I took a second to catch my breath. I grabbed my throat but it felt like his fingers were still there. I was gasping but it wasn't enough. My vision blurred, and I felt myself passing out.

"I told you what would happen if you interfered again," he said.

All I could feel was the dampness of the rocks under me, and the sharp edges pushing on my shirt and my skirt and my bare legs.

I opened my eyes and although the sun partially blocked my vision, I could make out Daddy standing over me. I began to scream as loudly as I could but I knew it was futile. I tried to stand up, but when Daddy pushed me down I hit my head on the rocks of the riverbank. A sticky wet pool of blood thickened my hair, and all I could think of was *This is it. Daddy killed Mama, and I was next*. I felt the cold steel of a knife to my throat.

Still struggling to stand, I realized I couldn't. Sharp pain prohibited me from getting up from the riverbank, and I was no match for Daddy's brute strength. All I could think was, *Here I come, Mama. Wait for me.*

ELIZABETH

I started to scream, a scream that never ended. The sound of the river rushing in my ears, the wind coming off the water, and Daddy's drunken curses filled my ears. Where was Henry? Was nobody going to stop this?

"Shut up, girl," Daddy sneered.

Then blinding pain filled my world. Over and over he hit me in the face, until I didn't scream anymore. It was as if I was floating outside of my body, looking down on the scene below. Again and again, the blows came, and somewhere far away I heard his voice, smelled the whiskey on his breath as he whispered in my ear, "Do you remember what I told you would happen if you didn't learn your place?" His hand touched my face, almost tenderly, then he grabbed my hair in his hand, his wild demonic eyes looking into mine crazily.

"No, Daddy," I begged, hating the sound of my voice, hating how weak and utterly powerless I sounded.

He laughed, cruelly, from deep within his chest. Suddenly, he didn't sound drunk anymore. It was as if he had sobered up instantly. I struggled against him, kicking him as hard as I could, but I was no match for his strength and weight. He was just too heavy.

"Hey! What's going on?" I heard a voice call.

Startled, Daddy lowered the knife away from my neck. When he turned to see who was speaking, I saw a figure, only darkly, standing a little ways off from the riverbank, but the noonday sun blocked my vision.

"You go on and mind your business," Daddy said, his voice echoed off the white bluffs.

"Let her go, Jonas!"

The voice sounded familiar through my pain, but it was hard to tell who it was. My ears were ringing from the blows Daddy had given me, and the blood flowing from my head clouded my vision.

Daddy grabbed me, and held the knife to my throat again, the edge scraped the soft skin of my neck.

I cried out in pain. The next thing I heard was the sound of someone rushing toward us, heavy footsteps on the sharp rocks of the riverbank. The crunch of gravel, the guttural groan of bodies falling, and the sounds of a struggle permeated my mind. Somewhere in my haze, I realized Daddy didn't have me anymore. His knife was in his fist, and he struggled to stab his pursuer, but Daddy had met his match. I couldn't see who it was who was fighting Daddy, partially because the one on top kept alternating between the man and Daddy, and partially because I could barely see with my bloody vision. There was a long time lapse between my thoughts and actions, and it felt as if I was swimming in a sea of pain.

When my thoughts caught up to my actions, I realized what to do. I searched around frantically for a good-sized rock, as big as I could hold, then I waited for Daddy to get the upper hand in the fight. When he did, I lifted the rock unsteadily and drove it down onto his head. It only took one blow, and Daddy collapsed onto my rescuer.

With a primeval groan, my rescuer pushed Daddy off of him.

I didn't look to see who had helped me; I just continued to bludgeon Daddy with the rock. Over and over, I brought the rock down on his head. Blood oozed out behind him on the rocks, and his eyes stared up at me blankly in death. Still I didn't stop. Soon, my tears mingled with his blood and the sobs became more and more retching, seeming to come from my soul.

"Elizabeth."

I heard a voice from somewhere behind me, but I didn't stop.

"Elizabeth, enough, he's gone."

Smooth, gentle arms wrapped around me, and the strength of them forced me to drop the rock on the ground next to Daddy's bleeding frame. When I turned around, tears and blood staining my face, I saw him. Antonio. His dark hair a mess, left eye blackened and swollen, his suit torn and disheveled. I had never seen him look that bad. His eyes met mine for a second, and we stood there breathing heavily from the exertion. My heart was beating right out of my chest it seemed, and my clothes were torn.

Antonio came to me in a single stride, his arms around me, his lips on my hair. "Oh my *Cara*," he murmured in my hair, "what was he going to do to you? What would he have done if I hadn't come?" He ran his fingers through his hair, and studied my face. "We have to get you out of here, now. My man's in the car, up at your place, but you can't walk, can you?" He asked a million questions at once.

He picked me up in one fell swoop and carried me out to the water. Tenderly he washed the blood from my hair, my skin, my fingernails. The water was cold but not frigid, but still I found myself freezing.

"I'll go up and get him, and we'll take care of him in a minute." He gestured to Daddy, who remained face down on the river rocks, motionless.

"Wait here," Antonio commanded, his voice thicker with his accent than usual. I sank down on the rock and began to shiver. He appeared alert. "You're going into shock," he said, mildly panicked. He took off his jacket and gave it to me. It was big on my shoulders, but it was warm. "*Cara*, I'll be right back, okay?" He gently slid a finger under my chin, lifting may face up to his.

I nodded, then he hurried through the woods as fast as he could.

I began to sob, and Antonio's associate picked me up and put me into the backseat of his car. Antonio told his friend to go take care of it, and he took me, not to a hospital, but a house in the middle of the woods where his private doctor tended to me for three days.

Antonio's "associate" then filled Daddy's body cavities with concrete. In the middle of the night, he dumped him into the War Eagle River. I didn't know this until many years later.

Nobody filed a missing persons report on him. Who would? Carolyn, who'd threatened to kill him if he came back? Mama? His boss, from a job he didn't have? When people talked about it later, they thought he just left town in a huff, and that he'd probably come back if he didn't find work in a field later.

Antonio, through his line of work, knew how to cover his tracks. In addition to making a huge contribution to the new governor's election fund, he remembered to go back to the house and leave a note for anyone that might stop by and check on me, saying that I had gone to visit my aunt in Tulsa. That was a good cover story because Henry didn't know her and Billy couldn't check up on it since he was being deployed to Africa.

I worried about Henry's feelings. I knew he would probably be hurt by the fact that he thought I had just run away and left him without explanation. But I couldn't tell him the truth.

This was a secret I kept with me always, Sammie. Many nights came when I woke up in a sweat, remembering Daddy's face when he died, and it haunted me, but I took comfort in the fact that at least he couldn't hurt anyone else.

When I recovered well enough to go home, about a month later, Antonio came into the bedroom of the place I was staying to drive me. All my clothes were gone from that horrible day, and everything I wore was new and designer. Antonio had driven to Tulsa to find me new clothes for a couple of reasons. He didn't want to be seen shopping for a woman that nobody had seen in a few weeks, and he didn't really think the clothes in Arkansas were anything to write home about. My wardrobe was a hundred times more than it had been. I had at least a dozen dresses of different styles and functions, from simple to formal, along with accessories: purses and handbags of different sizes and styles, along with inexpensive costume jewelry to boot. It might have been inexpensive as far as Antonio was concerned, but some of it cost more money than I had ever seen. I tried to argue with him that I didn't need that stuff, but he wouldn't budge on the issue. I saw the stubborn side that made people not argue with him.

I'll never forget what I was wearing the day I went back to the cabin. An emerald green dress with embroidery along the bottom of the skirt, and simple buttons going down the front. The collar was low enough to show my collarbone, and the dress fit snugly and perfectly. How Antonio guessed my exact size and measurements, I never knew. He was just good with fashion, obviously, but to choose something that looked so good on me. I barely recognized the person staring back at me in the mirror. I resembled some kind of high-class college girl. My hair had been cut and styled, Antonio had seen to that. When I protested he told me it would help our cover story of me going to Tulsa if I came back looking like I had been on vacation.

I was packing up the clothes into some simple but elegant suitcases that he had purchased for me, when I saw him standing in the hallway. He was leaning against the doorframe, his arms crossed, smiling at me. He looked taller and more handsome than ever in his gray linen suit and tie, his white shirt buttoned and starched, accenting his tanned skin. Of course, he was immaculate, as if he had stepped out of the pages of a fashion magazine.

"Mmmm. Elizabeth, you look wonderful," he said, smiling and showing his perfect teeth. He walked over to me and put his arms around my waist.

The smell of him, manly but clean, and the aroma of an expensive cologne filled my nose, dizzying my senses. He held me in his arms like a child, and I couldn't help but rest my head on his shoulder. He was so easy to melt into. I felt his lips on my hair, and then I felt his hands on my face, soft and manicured, when he pressed his lips gently to mine. Somewhere in the recesses of my mind, I felt guilty. I pulled away from his embrace, and though I tried not to meet his gaze, his dark brown eyes demanded I look up. I saw hurt there, and an ember of anger, but it was quickly covered up by his cool veneer.

"What's wrong? Am I reading signals that aren't there?" he asked, his eyes searching.

I knew I must be crazy to rebuff him. This man had my father disposed of only a few weeks before without ever laying a finger on him.

"I-I'm sorry, but—" I paused, trying to find the words. "I appreciate all you've done, but I need to go home."

His eyes grew guarded. "Of course Elizabeth," his voice smooth as velvet and quiet as a memory. "I think I know what this is about."

My breath caught, and I struggled to slow down my heartbeat. He sat down on the side of the bed. "You are worried about my intentions, because we are alone together in this bedroom," he said, gesturing to the room. "You needn't worry, my *Cara*," he said with a grin. "I'll not attack you like an animal." He smoothed the sheet next to him absentmindedly.

"Oh, no, that's not what I think," I started, the words falling from my lips like pebbles from the side of the mountain. "I know you are a gentleman."

"Yes, that's true, I am," he admitted, "but that doesn't mean that I'm not a man without needs, and desires." His eyes met mine, and I saw his hunger for me there. "I am old-fashioned, however, and my mother has raised me right. So I'll not ask to have you unless you are my wife," he said, and then, in one swift motion, he was on bended knee in front of me, holding a small velvet box.

My hand went to my chest, and my eyes widened in surprise. He opened the box to show a single perfect diamond in a golden setting. The stone seemed to reflect every beam of sunlight in the room and shone magnificently.

"Elizabeth, will you marry me?" He spoke the simple words, his velvety accent magnifying their beauty a hundred times over. "I want you to come away with me, far from this town. You don't belong here in Arkansas. I am moving back to Florence, and I want to take you with me. You are smart and beautiful, and I want us to be happy together, and to have many children with your copper hair and wit. I will take care of you, and if you want to go to college and study literature and poetry, I can make that happen. We can sit outside and watch the sun go down in Florence every night, with our children playing safely in my family's vineyard. It will be a beautiful life."

How he made it sound. Lovely, uncomplicated. I would never want for anything again. What woman wouldn't take an offer such as this? To have a beautiful, cultured husband that offered everything you every wanted up on a single golden, not silver, platter. Except for a few minor problems.

First of all, his business dealings scared me. I had only seen some of it come to play through a medicated haze over a couple of weeks, but it was shady. I learned that nobody said no to Antonio. Sure, he loved me then when I was young and beautiful and exciting, but what happened when I was old and not so beautiful and exciting anymore? What happened if he didn't like something I did, or said? I couldn't imagine he would be violent like Daddy was, I never had seen him that way with women at all, but the fear would always be there. And I really had no desire to be the little wife that was kept in the dark about her husband's business dealings. I never wanted to be in the dark about anything.

There I was, being handed a romantic proposition by a beautiful man that had cleaned up my mess at a critical time, and all I could think of was Henry. How he must have been hurt when I left, and how he was probably angry. How he was probably reading his bible daily, praying, searching for answers within the pages on why I left without saying anything. It broke my heart. All I could think of was going to him. But what would I say? How would I explain?

I don't know how long we stayed like that, Antonio on one knee, holding the ring, and me not taking it. Finally, he rose to his feet. "Elizabeth, what is this? Don't you love me? Don't you want to be my wife?"

I swallowed hard, and saw the faint shine of tears in his eyes, and felt the same in mine. "Antonio, I—"

"Listen, I can't stay here. The cops have been getting suspicious, not about your father, but about the moonshining. I have to go back to my country. Especially with this war getting so heated up, I am afraid if I don't go now, I will never get to go back. My mother is ill, and I need to go to her. I was hoping I could take you there and marry you in a beautiful ceremony with all my family there to see."

"I can't," I said, and in his eyes I saw the storm cloud brewing.

"Why? Don't you love me?"

"I . . . love somebody else," I said the words for the first time.

Hurt, then anger, passed through his eyes like a thunderstorm. He closed the box with the ring in it with a snap.

"I see. Henry, right? You are gonna leave me for some hayseed preacher?" His lips were tight against his teeth. "I can give you so much more than he can. Do you really want to live with him in poverty the rest of your life, here in this little town where nothing happens?"

"Antonio, I am grateful for all you've done for me, and I do think I love you, it's just . . . I don't want to leave Arkansas. This is my home."

He sat down on the bed again, and ran his fingers through his coal black hair. He glanced up at me with a tiny smile around his lips. "I understand. Stupid me, I should have never have left you alone so much. I knew if I turned my back, someone else will snatch you up. Come on, I'll drive you home."

Antonio had had the cabin cleaned and the pantry stocked for me. He'd had his associate, Frank, bring in my new clothes, and before he left he kissed my cheek and said, "My *Cara*, if you change your mind." He left a sheet of paper with an address in Italy on it. And with that, he was gone.

I stood there for a moment in the kitchen. I felt like I had been gone forever. Everything looked different, but at the same time everything appeared the same. The old furniture looked older, Mama's rocking chair in the corner with a quilt over it, the old couch against the wall, the hand-carved kitchen table Mama said her daddy had made in 1888, and the old brass bed that Mama had died in across the divided curtain. I felt lonely in the cabin by myself.

I took my heels off and took a walk down to the river barefoot. It was summer now, the water was clear and cold, and ran across the smooth river rocks as if in a hurry. The waterfalls were frothy and white from the motion, and I could see fish leaping. The moss growing near the water was bright green, the color of Mama's eyes, and the sky a lovely cloudless indigo. I felt a chill in my bones when I saw the last place Daddy took a breath. Antonio's associate had done a thorough job. There was not a single drop of blood on the rocks, or any sign of struggle anywhere. I decided not to linger there and began walking down the riverbank. Then I saw him.

Henry was casting his pole deep into the river. A faded brown cowboy hat pushed low over his brow to keep out the sunlight was the first thing I noted. His huge frame, and his long, tanned arms, sprinkled with freckles, was the second, and I noticed the ripple of his muscles as he set the pole down between two rocks. He was shirtless in the summer heat, and a thin glimmer of sweat dampened his skin. His chest was perfectly carved and he'd tied the shirt he'd been wearing around his narrow waist. His shorts fit perfectly, and his legs that seemed to be carved out of stone were tanned and covered with a layer of golden hair that seemed to glint in the sun. His feet were bare, and I knew the rocks didn't hurt them because they had been toughened up long ago.

He picked up the next fishing pole, and even from where I stood, I could see his calloused hands because he worked hard in the fields with his daddy, because he hunted and fished and was a manly man. Suddenly, the sight of Henry seemed ten times sexier than Antonio ever had been. I felt the old familiar quickening of my heart at the sight of him.

As if he heard it too, he turned to me. He smiled, almost reluctantly, and turned back to his fishing. "Hey," he said simply, not meeting my eyes again.

"Hey," I said quietly.

Neither of us talked for a while. I sat down on my rock, and Henry expertly baited his next pole silently. The calm, clear water rippled gently from a summer breeze that blew off the shoreline.

"I've missed you," I whispered.

"I was hurt when you didn't let me know your plans. You know, friends let each other know where they are," he said, paying a lot of attention to the water, and pushing his hat down even lower over his eyes.

"Is that what we are, Henry?" I asked, feeling a little panicked. "Just friends?" I stood up and was next to him in just a few seconds. I could smell him, and, oh, how the scent was different from Antonio's. He wore aftershave too, but probably just something he bought at the store in town. He smelled a little like sweat, not odor, but sweat, and of fresh air and outdoors and sunshine. He smelled like heaven.

He put the fishing pole down and faced me. "Honestly, Elizabeth, I don't know what we are." His voice was short and his brow wrinkled, his expression hauntingly honest. "I don't know who you are either," he said, motioning to my dress. "You stand here before me in some fancy dress you bought in Tulsa, looking like a movie star and too sexy for your own good, and certainly too good to stay here at this hick town with me."

I felt the sting and the compliment all at once. Me, sexy? Me, a movie star?

"You run off, not telling anybody where you're goin' or when you're comin' back."

I had to smile, not because I relished his pain, but because whenever he got emotional, his accent came in full force.

"And all I can think of is, 'I'm a little late for a date and she takes off?'"

I took a breath in. Of course. He'd never showed that day, and Daddy had.

He took off his hat and threw it onto the riverbank. His hair, messy and wild from being under a hat all morning, and his blond curls stuck to his forehead crazily.

I smiled, and reached up with my fingers to move a strand from his eyes.

His hand caught my wrist, and he gripped it gently. "Don't, Elizabeth," he said, closing his eyes. "Don't touch me if you don't mean it. I can't stand it anymore."

I waited for him to open his eyes, and then I stood on tiptoes and wrapped my arms around his neck. I pressed my lips on his, and though he stood there rigidly for a second, he melted and placed his massive arms around my waist, drawing me to him. His kisses were passionate and fervent, and his lips moved from my mouth to my neck, and he seemed to bury his face there.

"What happened? Why did you leave?"

I stood there for a moment, then said, "Henry, I can't tell you everything now. Maybe I can't tell you everything ever. Can you trust me that it was necessary I go away? It had nothing to do with you being late that day."

"It was your daddy, wasn't it?" His eyes bored into mine.

My breath caught. How could he know that? I found myself nodding. If I could trust anyone with my secret, it was him.

I sat down on the rock, and he sat next to me. I told him the story, but I didn't start from a few days ago, I started back before Delilah was born. I told him what Daddy had done to Mama, and what he threatened to do to me. I told him everything that had happened the last year, all the way from what happened an hour before. He quietly listened, not interrupting me until I became quiet myself. I didn't look him in the eye, I only focused on the water.

He raised it to his lips. He kissed my palm, and then placed my hand on his chest, burying my small hand in both of his. He said quietly, "Elizabeth, I'm sorry I wasn't here to help you. And as much as I dislike Antonio, I'm glad he was there to save your life. One of the kids got hurt and I had to find the doc to set a broken arm. When I got here it was nightfall, and I went to your place the next morning and you weren't there. I thought you had finally ran off with Antonio to get married."

"I couldn't marry Antonio," I said, resting my head on my shoulder. "I don't love him. I love you."

"You don't know how long I've waited for you to say that." Henry leaned over and kissed me again. "I love you, too, Elizabeth."

"You love me, even after what I just told you I did to my father?" My eyes welled with tears.

"Elizabeth, he never would have stopped had you not done what you had to. I don't judge you for that. I judge myself for not being there to take care of you. I don't ever want that to happen again."

I kissed him for what seemed like an eternity, then I said, "Henry, will you marry me?"

His face broke out in a grin, and he took off his cowboy hat and threw it up with a shout.

"I wish you hadn't stole my thunder, but I'll take you up on that offer!" He laughed, his big boisterous Henry laugh, and scooped me up into his arms and spun me around.

"We were married for 48 happy years, and we had four children. All of our lives we spent here in Arkansas, and they were happy ones. Your Grandpa Henry loved us, and taught us by example how God cares for us, and it's because of him that I believe.

We felt troubled by the way Diane turned to drugs, and how she neglected your mother, but I thought we made up for that, at least a little, when she came to live with us.

The point is, Sam, there have been generations of strong women before you and, God willing, generations after. I've told you my secrets, the deep dark ones of the past that I only shared with my dear Henry, so that maybe, just maybe, you will tell us your secrets so we can help you. I know you have a secret you are not telling anyone, and that is why you are in such pain these days. Know that we love you and will accept you no matter what. I don't care what the secret is. It doesn't matter. We love you. Come back to us."

Suddenly, after the last words came, I felt so very tired. My head hurt horribly, and I knew I should probably tell one of the nurses, but I didn't want to. I laid my head down on Sam's pillow next to her, so close my hair and her hair were intertwined. I decided nobody would probably care if I took a little nap by my Sammie.

When I was lying there, I had a dream. I was meandering down a country road, the one that went to my cabin, but it was different. It was the way it used to when Henry was alive, and all the wildflowers were in bloom. At the end of the road, I saw Samantha. She was standing in a yellow sundress, barefoot on the country road, her red hair the color of autumn. While we were embracing, I saw my Henry, just as he was on our wedding day. I felt happy to see him, but at the same time, concerned. Why was he so young, when I was so old?

I glanced down at my hands, expecting to see what I usually did: pale, wrinkled skin, covered in age spots, but, instead, I saw the hands of a young woman, with my beautiful wedding ring on my left hand, just as it should be. I held my hands out in front of me, comparing them and I realized I was wearing my wedding dress. My hair was red, not white, and I was young again.

Henry saw me, broke out into a grin, and held his arms open to me. I told Sam, "Samantha, you need to go back that way, the way I have just come from. Everybody is waiting for you." She kissed my cheek, and did what she was told.

After I saw her safely down the road, I ran to Henry's arms, because I was young and vibrant, and because I could.

Chapter 12

EDEN

I got off the elevator and saw pure chaos outside of Sam's room. My heart jumped up into my throat. "What's happening?" I cried, pushing through the crowd of people that were in front of Sam's room. I heard the sounds of a code: someone called orders for Epi, someone yelled "Clear!" the sound of the crash cart's defibrillator doing its job. That's when I saw it wasn't Sam they were coding, it was Nana.

Sister Agatha was standing with her clipboard, which she laid down on a side table. She came over to me and put her hand on my shoulder.

"I'm so sorry, child," she said. "They found her blue and unresponsive, laying her head next to your daughter."

Sister and I knew each other well. I had called her many a time for that same situation, only it'd always been somebody else.

I burst into tears. How could I lose them both? I couldn't bear it.

Someone came up behind me and put his arms around me I knew it wasn't Craig. This man was too big, plus he wore scrubs. I looked up, square into Mike's face.

SAMANTHA

I was alone again, back on the dirt road, leaving the mountaintop. The woman was not with me anymore. The trees that were green and lush and blooming in their springtime regalia were now in the wardrobe of autumn: ambers and chocolates, crimson and gingers. As I continued down the road, a few here and there fell softly to the ground. There was a cool breeze blowing across my face and suddenly I felt alone and afraid.

But then I saw Nana. Except, it's not Nana as I knew her. It was a younger Nana, she seemed hardly older than me. But I knew it was her. She came over to me and gave me a hug and a kiss. She told me I was going the wrong way, that I should follow the road back home. When she began to leave, I watched a man hold his arms open for her, and soon their fingers were entwined as they strolled in the opposite direction down the road. Nana turned one more time to me before she left. "Remember, Samantha, we are War Eagle Women. We fight."

I always listened to Nana, even if I didn't listen to anyone else.

I heard voices calling my name. "Sam, Sam, wake up," they urged me. But I was too tired to wake up. My eyes were open already as the red clay road unfolded before me. *Why do they want me to wake up? I am not asleep.*

I could hear my mother's voice, trying to persuade me. Why wouldn't she leave me alone? At the same time, I missed her. I hadn't seen her in a long time. Why had I been alone for so long?

"Open your eyes, Sam!" my mother's voice persistently commanded.

Don't they understand? My eyes were open. Maybe they were not open enough. Really, I just wanted to sleep. I wanted to lie down in the meadow and not wake up. Maybe if I showed them my eyes were open, they would let me rest. I opened them as wide as I could.

The light was blinding. My mother's face, the most beautiful face I knew, was leaning over me. Why was she crying? I didn't really want to talk right then. There was a man standing next to her. I thought he was a doctor judging by his lab coat, scrubs, and stethoscope.

"Well, hey, Samantha," the doctor said cheerfully. He was shining a light in my eyes. "Welcome back."

I tried to speak but nothing happened.

A nurse said, "Sam, you can't talk. Do you know where you are?"

I shook my head no.

"You are in the hospital, Sam. I'm Jennifer. I've been taking care of you. Right now you have a tube in your mouth to help you breathe. We are going to take it out in a few minutes then you can talk, okay?" She smiled at me.

I liked her immediately because her eyes were kind. A bunch of people in scrubs came into my room. They were talking in hospital jargon to each other.

"Okay, Sam. This is it. I'm going to give you a little medicine in your I.V. and it might hurt a little to get the tube out because it's been in there a while."

A while? How long have I been here? What day is it?

"Okay, Sam, on the count of three: one, two, three."

With that, I felt my throat being scratched as if a truck was being driven through my esophagus. God, it hurt. I took a deep breath and everybody seemed pleased.

"Mom?" I asked, my voice scratchy from disuse.

Mom was standing next to me, holding my hand. Her eyes filled with tears as she looked over my head to the doctor on the other side of the bed. There was an expression that passed from him to her that I was not ready for.

"Yes, baby?" she said, rubbing my hand.

"What day is it?"

Mom sucked in her breath and blew it out. "Sam, it's your birthday."

My birthday?

The last thing I remembered was the party. When was that? Two months ago?

The monitor started to beep crazily as I realized how long I had been there. Somebody put some oxygen on my nose, then I saw it. A folded funeral program with my Nana's picture on it.

EDEN

Sam was doing all right now. She was upset by the news about Nana, understandably. She looked lost and grief-stricken. I wanted to kick myself for leaving that program out like that. But how was I supposed to know that Sam was going to spontaneously start trying to wake up after all this time?

I stepped out in the hallway to call Craig. I tried to call him earlier to tell him about the plan to extubate Sam but I couldn't reach him. Even now, I couldn't reach him. His cell phone rang and rang and just as it was going to voice mail I spotted him coming down the hallway. He was pacing the hallway nervously.

"Did they do it? Is she okay?" he asked.

In spite of myself, my heart went out to him. His hair was a mess, and it was obvious he just rolled out of bed.

"Yes. And Yes." I smiled. "She's awake, Craig! And she's talking."

Craig's eyes started to water and he hugged me. He started to really sob, and he didn't let go. Just then, Mike came out of the ICU doors. When he noticed Craig holding me, he stopped short and his smile faded. Suddenly his face went from casual to all business.

"She's doing fine, just fine," he reassured Craig, and then walked by us without another word. I could tell he was mad, but what was I supposed to do?

Craig stopped hugging me. "She's going to be okay, isn't she, Eden?"

I smiled, my eyes watering. "Yeah, I think she is." And for just a moment, one glorious moment, I let myself believe it. And then, I felt his lips on mine.

EDEN

Today I had to do the unthinkable. I had to go to Nana's cabin and put her things away. I would like to have waited on this, but I knew I couldn't. When Sam got out of the hospital, she would still need a lot of help, and I might not get back there. No, I needed to do this now.

I smoked all the way to the cabin. I must have smoked two packs just on the way. I hadn't smoked since Craig and I were together. Just being around him drove a person to smoke just to keep the edge off. But when he's not around, and I was in more control of my world so to speak, I didn't need the cigarettes.

I had the radio tuned to a classic rock station. Boston was on crooning "Amanda". Not my favorite big-hair ballad, but it would have to do. I cranked it up and lit another cigarette at the stoplight.

I had lost about ten pounds since Sam's been in the hospital. My pants were baggy, but not enough to justify buying new ones. I was able to do some laundry though, so at least I didn't look so rat assed as normal. My hair was pulled up in a messy ponytail, and I wore a button-up polo with a tank underneath, green and white, my favorite colors. My jeans, though loose, were still good, and my boots were black and leathery. Normally I didn't care about my clothes as much, but I knew I needed all the fortitude I could get when I went out to Nana's. And, sometimes, dressing up made me feel better.

The wild blackberry bushes had grown out over the clay road leading to Nana's. Of course, they weren't in bloom so they were just inconvenient. I almost missed the turnoff when I saw the red mailbox that marked home. How could a place seem so forgotten?

I pulled up the gravel driveway and almost wept when I saw the rose bushes Nana had planted dying. Dead leaves covered the porch and the windows on the cabin were filthy. Without Nana's weekly washing the dust gathered quickly. The broad porch still stood as rustic as when my great-great-grandfather Jonas had built it. Nana had never felt the need to update when it looked fine. The logs had long since been treated with modern materials to preserve the wood, yet the cabin still held the same charm. You'd never know that the cabin that was over a hundred years old.

Papa Henry, as I called Nana's husband, had seen to it that the cabin had never fallen into disrepair while he was alive. More than once, he'd asked Nana if she wanted to move. He'd never made big money as a preacher, but he was careful with the money he had and when he died, Nana was more than taken care of.

But Nana didn't want to move. She'd lived her whole life in that cabin, and it was the place where her mother had died. In fact, Grandma Betty was buried less than a mile away in the family cemetery. Nana had said she couldn't bear to leave Grandma alone. So Papa had quit trying to get her to move. Instead, he renovated the cabin until it was better than ever.

The river, just to the back of the cabin, sang peacefully that day. A greenish blue, the water lapped the sides of the bluff. A lone hawk flew over the river, taking his time to lazily descend to a nearby branch.

Nana had told me countless times how much she loved that cabin and how much she loved that river. She spoke of the river as if it were a woman. I always laughed at her, but, standing in front of it without my Nana, I closed my eyes and listened. I could imagine that the river spoke to me as well.

I finally went into the cabin. Everything was neat as a pin, as I'd expected. Nana was a heck of a housekeeper. She believed in the motto 'A place for everything and everything in its place.' There was a comfortable couch against the window, and a pretty rug, probably handmade, covered the old wood floor. I decided I needed to make a fire to get the chill out of the air. When I went to the kitchen to find the lighter, I saw it. The manuscript that Nana had been working on. I made a pot of coffee and sat down to read.

Hours later, I glanced up at the clock, my face drenched in tears. The shadows on the floor told me that the sun was going down and I was going to have to stay late to pack up Nana's things. I hardly had the heart, but I needed to take care of this task.

Nana had left the manuscript unfinished. I wondered how she had done that. She had a computer but barely knew how to use one. Then I saw the number of a dictation service next to her phone. I decided to call them the next day to see if they were in some way helping my Nana write her memoirs.

I packed up Nana's things, one by one. Her clothes, few and comfortable, didn't take long. Her books were another story. So many volumes! I was overwhelmed with how I was going to deal with them, but I knew I couldn't sell a single one. I found her purse and when I emptied it, I discovered a miniature tape recorder. I pushed 'play', and listened to my dear Nana's voice as she told Samantha, unresponsive in a coma, all her secrets. I fast-forwarded to the end and what I heard gave me goose bumps.

"So I hope that helps you, Samantha, to tell your secret, the secret that is eating you up inside. I . . . have to go now. I see my Henry waiting for me. Please, please, don't belong in that place you've been to. It's my turn to go, and it's your turn to come back here, among the living. You've dawdled there too long."

Then I heard the tape recorder fall and turn off.

Chapter 13

SAMANTHA

I wanted to sleep more but I couldn't. The routine of the hospital was getting to me. All I could think about was Nana and how she wasn't there anymore. And some strange dream I had about her a long time ago. Nana in a wedding dress, and telling me which way to go on a road I was walking on. I wanted to ask her about it, but I couldn't. The thought tore me up, and I didn't feel well.

About seven, a change of shift happened and I heard the day shift nurses coming in to replace the night shift. About 7:30, they brought breakfast: a glob of watery scrambled eggs, toast as cold as a tombstone, tepid coffee, cement-like oatmeal, a half of a tasteless orange. I can only manage a few bites before I left like vomiting. I tried to drink the warm milk at least, but it just wasn't happening.

Brittney, the day-shift nurse, came to check on me. I really didn't like her. She was too perky, too sweet, her platinum-blond hair too perfect. She reminded me of iced tea when you put in too much Equal; syrupy and artificial, a promise of sweet but a delivery of fake.

"Hello, Miss Sam," Brittney said, opening the blinds.

The light beams cut through the blinds in even slices, making my eyes squint. "Close the blinds, please," I croaked, trying to be civil.

"Nope, it's too dark in here, and you need to be awake more. You have physical therapy today."

"Pass," I said, pushing my breakfast tray away. I had about five different bracelets on my hand. They reminded me of dog tags.

"Oh, I'm afraid that's not an option," Brittney chirped annoyingly, it reminded me of those birds on the window in the scene on *Mary Poppins*, phony and animatronic.

"I'm the patient here, and I have rights, and I am refusing physical therapy."

Brittney ignored me and started to clear my tray away, but stopped when she noticed how little I had eaten.

"Don't you want to finish your food? You've barely eaten anything the past few days." She frowned, her perfect white teeth hidden behind her perfectly made-up lips.

"Calling this slop food is a bit of a stretch, don't ya think so, *Brit*?" I said, deliberately shortening her name, even though she has asked me repeatedly not to.

"Okay, I'm just going to lay it all out on the line for you, Sam," Brittney said, all of the fake cheeriness gone. "If you don't do physical therapy, you won't learn to walk on your own again, and you won't get to go home. About the not eating"—she pushed the tray forward—"if you can't do better than this, we may have to put the tube back in you and force you. You're supposed to be gaining weight, not losing it."

I laughed at that one. "Gaining weight? What are you talking about? Obviously the recycled air is getting to you. I've done nothing but gain weight since I've been here!" I sit forward, and angrily yank up my gown exposing my fat belly. "See this!" I spit out angrily. "What do you call this!"

Brittney did a double-take, and then rubbed her temple with her forefinger and thumb. She sat down, uninvited, on the edge of my bed.

With the exception of the monitors beeping, the silence stretched.

"You seriously think you've been gaining weight?" Brittney finally asked.

"Wow, I'm knew there was a health care crisis and all, but I thought you had to have a certain I.Q. to finish nursing school, but I guess—"

She held her hand, palm facing me.

A feeling of dread overpowers me, so thick I can't breathe. Then she says the words.

"Sam, you're not fat. You're pregnant."

EMILY

Sam was awake now, and I had given her a few days to come around, but today I had to go talk to her. We don't have a lot in common, but I really think she can help me with my issues with Spencer. She didn't like him very much, but I thought she could give me some advice. Sometimes if I asked her opinion, it made sense. And I knew she of all people wouldn't be drooling over Spencer like the other girls, or try to come between us so she could have him.

Sam hated him. Usually, if I even brought up his name, she rolled her eyes and left the room. I still couldn't believe he broke up with me. I haven't slept since it happened. I hadn't eaten either. Pretty much, I just lay around in bed crying. Yesterday, I tried to go to practice, because I was in danger of getting cut from Friday night's performance if I didn't. We were doing our routine, and I saw Spencer, up in the bleachers, his arm around Jessica Myers. I was at the top of the pyramid, and I started to feel dizzy. When I saw him kiss her, I lost my balance.

Suddenly the ground sped to meet me, but at the last second two of the girls caught me. I told them I was sick and needed to go home.

On the way out, I saw Spencer's truck parked in the lot under the oak tree.

I let all of the air out of his tires.

EDEN

The drive back to the Prior house was quiet. There was a Journey song playing on the radio. Bruce reached over and turned off the radio. "Eden, I . . ." he began, but the words choked up in his throat. "I don't even know what to say, how to begin." The blackened highway, edged with snow, rolled out before us.

"You don't have to say anything, Bruce." I tried to comfort him. "You don't have to worry about anything now." I smiled in the darkness.

"Of course I have to worry! I just cheated on my wife. I broke my wedding vows!" he raged, yelling at me. "Stupid, so stupid!" He pounded his fists hard on the steering wheel with so much force I thought it would break. He began to cry.

I didn't expect that. A feeling of dread welled up inside of me. Was Bruce going to hate me now?

We stopped at a red light. The only sound was his sobbing and the blinker on his truck. Outside, sleet was falling on the windshield, the wet snow and ice mixture making a scratching sound on the frozen glass.

"Hey, it's okay." I reached over and ran my fingers through his hair.

In one second, his hand was gripping my wrist, harder than necessary. "No, it's not okay. Don't touch me, Eden. Don't ever touch me again," he said, and he threw my arm into my lap. On the right side of the road a 'Caution, falling rocks' sign became illuminated for a short few seconds as we passed.

Caution, falling rocks.

If they only knew.

Chapter 14

SAMANTHA

I'm pregnant. And, apparently, the last to know. How could this have happened? I couldn't believe nobody has asked me any questions about it. Maybe they were waiting for me to get better first.

Today, a social worker named Amy Jordan, a young, pretty, brown-haired lady with big green eyes, came into my room with my mother. Mom sat down on the side of my bed, glancing at me with her kind, understanding expression. I hated when she did that. I mean, I wasn't a lab specimen. I wasn't a zoo exhibit. And I wasn't someone to be pitied.

"Hi, Sam." Mom smiled at me and leaned over to give me a kiss. She smelled of White Shoulders and sunshine. I never thought I would miss the sunshine.

"Hi, Mom. What's all this?" I asked.

"Samantha, I'm Amy. I'm a social worker at the hospital here." The woman had gentle eyes and smooth skin and smelled like orchid perfume. Her long brown hair was up in a ponytail, and she was wearing a white long-sleeved button-up shirt, perfectly creased, with black slacks and gorgeous black flats. For color, she had a turquoise scarf around her neck.

"How nice for you," I sneered. "Now if you wouldn't mind, I was just getting ready to take a nap. I'm bushed."

"This will only take a moment." She smiled. It was a real smile, one that was meant to con me into trusting her.

Well, forget it.

"Samantha, don't be rude. You need to listen to her. She's here to help you."

"Help me? With what?"

"Sam," Amy began, smoothing out the sheet on my bed, "we need to talk to you about your pregnancy."

"Um, I'd rather not."

"It's not just going to go away, dear. You need to make plans." Amy glances from me to my mother.

I had never in my life seen Mom so nervous. She was actually sweating.

"Well, don't worry," I said. "I've already decided what to do."

"What's that?" Mom asked.

I noticed she was picking at her cuticles like she did when she was worried. "I'm going to get rid of it."

Mom sucked in her breath sharply. The room went silent. The sound of the clock ticking grew deafening. A look I couldn't quite identify passed between Amy and my mother.

"I'm afraid that's not possible," Amy said.

At that point I became really angry. Had my mother suddenly become mute? Did she have to rely on a stranger to talk to me about my "options"? Why did we need that woman anyway?

"Why not? Is this not America? Land of the free, home of the brave, and all that jazz? Did I, along with my memory, suddenly wake up in a third world country or something? What are you talking about?"

"Sam, when they brought you in, you were already ten weeks pregnant."

"And?" I asked impatiently.

"Sam, you have been in the hospital for seventeen weeks."

I must have given her the deer in the headlights look, because she paused before continuing.

"You are twenty-seven weeks pregnant with your baby girl. It's too late."

As if on cue, I felt the baby move inside of me.

EDEN

I tried to talk to Sam, but she wouldn't have it. Her eyes, dark and vacant, it frightened me. The sounds of the hospital comforted me; they were sounds that I was familiar with. The quiet beeping of the monitor, the compressing of the blood pressure cuff on Sam's arm, clicking and relaxing, the ticking of the clock marked the passing of minutes into hours as I sat in that old vinyl recliner, trying to concentrate on the patchwork quilt I had brought up there to keep my hands and mind busy.

Sam turned restlessly from side-to-side, now and then crying in her sleep. I tried to hold her, to tell her everything was going to be okay, but she pushed me away violently and hissed at me to leave her alone. So I did.

The ticking of the clock reminded me just how quickly time flies, though it seemed to not fly at all at that moment. That moment seems to linger, quietly, painfully. A few weeks ago we rented the movie *Click*, where a man fast-forwards over the annoying and uncomfortable moments of his life, but ultimately realizes that there were golden times in the bad as well as the good. I was hard pressed at that moment to find a single golden nugget, but it always seemed that way.

After Bruce and I had slept together, it changed everything. Of course, being older, I realized that sex always changed the dynamic of a relationship, but back then, I wasn't sure what I had expected to happen once I had "won" my game and seduced Bruce. He avoided me more than ever, and spent a lot of time working overtime at his job. He never spoke to me except to say, "Pass the potatoes." He never looked me in the eye either. One day, at dinner, when the only sounds were the clink of the silverware on Joy's mother's china, she all of a sudden announced, "Okay. That's it."

Startled, Bruce glanced up at Joy. "What are you talking about?"

For a minute, I noticed a light flush in his cheeks and a bit of sweat on his brow.

"Oh, I think you and Eden both know what I'm referring to," she went on, the expression on her face was hard to read.

The acid in my stomach seemed to double, and I felt my palms grow wet. I wanted to say something, but my voice wouldn't work. The back of my throat seemed to be full of sawdust.

Joy's short brown hair seemed even more matronly as she sat on her side of the table, her blue eyes serious.

"What I mean, what I want to talk to you about it, is what the heck is going on between the two of you?"

The room became deathly quiet. "Mom, what are you talking about?" Sarah asked, frowning.

Cody seemed worried as he made a river with his gravy and busied himself by dunking his roll into it like a boat.

Joy stood up, put her hands on her hips and rolled her eyes. "What I mean is, something has obviously happened between the two of you. And it's affecting the entire family. Look at us," she went on, her serious eyes touching on each face. "Nobody has said a single word since we sat down at this table tonight."

That was the truth. Before, dinners at the Prior household used to be pretty lively, everybody talked over each other, good-natured teasing, bad jokes, and the whole nine yards. Since the incident with Bruce, and the fact he could hardly look me in the eye, the strain was showing. Joy thought there had been some sort of falling out, which there had, of course, but nothing she could pinpoint.

"What's going on with you all?" she asked, arms crossed.

"Nothing," Bruce mumbled.

"Well, whatever it is, ya'll need to clear it up. This is torture for all of us, and I won't have it," Joy added, sitting down at the table finally. She leaned over to me, and put the stake through my heart when she said, "Eden, I know I am being tough with you as well, but that is because as far as I am concerned, you are a part of this family, too, and so I plan to treat you as part of the family and kick your butt if necessary."

At that, Cody laughed as if he couldn't believe his mother said, "Butt." Sarah smiled, too, and I managed to plaster a fake smile for her benefit. But inside, I felt like dying.

How were we supposed to "clear it up," I wanted to know. Unless I could somehow go back in time and put my virginity back into place, I didn't see a way of that happening. I pretended to be very, very interested in Joy's meatloaf.

After dinner that night, the phone rang. Joy was washing dishes, with me drying, and she put down the pot scrubber, wiped her hands on her apron, and answered the phone. Something the caller said made her face go pale. She said something I couldn't hear, then came back into the kitchen.

"Eden, get your purse," she said, leaving the dishes. "Something's wrong with your mother."

My heartfelt a hundred pounds in my chest, too fat and awkward to beat properly. What was wrong with Mom?

Chapter 15

SAMANTHA

The fact that I was pregnant was bad, of course. The fact that it was too late to abort was even worse. I felt certain that if I could get out of this Catholic hospital I could find somebody that would do late-term abortions. There was no way I wanted this baby. In fact, I didn't want her inside of me, sucking away my life, my opportunities, my blood, my soul.

The funny thing was, nobody had bothered to ask me if it was Matt's. I guessed they just assumed it was since he was the last in the long parade of losers I'd hung out with those past few months. Since Matt was dead, he wasn't around to argue with the consensus. I guessed I would just let them think what they wanted.

"Samantha?"

I heard a voice at the doorway. It was a big, muscular, tanned guy with kind green eyes framed by stylish glasses. His curly dark hair was in the messy-spiked style and he had a bit of a goatee.

"Well, since I'm the one in the hospital gown, you must be a quick one."

He chuckled. "Your friend Brittney told me about you, to watch out for that biting wit. She was not kidding!" He wrote something down on his clipboard.

"Brittney, my friend? Sadly I have misinterpreted your intelligence." I knew I was being petty, unreasonable. So sue me.

"Actually, that was *my* attempt at wit. I came by yesterday and saw you throw some fuzzy socks at her when she was nagging you to eat."

"She was lucky. Next time it will be the bedpan."

At that, he laughed a loud, boisterous laugh that startled some nuns who were walking by.

I noticed his perfect white teeth. Okay, he wasn't ugly. Not at all. And, he didn't seem much older than me. Probably fresh out of school.

"I forgot to introduce myself. I'm Chris, the physical therapist assistant."

"Chris? That's unfortunate. Your mom must not have been very creative."

"Actually, I'd say *you* are the one who is not creative, if you are *really* resorting to 'your mama' jokes right now."

That time I didn't smile. I laughed.

And it felt pretty good.

"Let's get you up for a bit. I'll take you on the grand tour of the post-op floor," Chris said, as he moved my tray out of the way and handed me a robe. He didn't seem like he would take 'no' for an answer.

When he held his hand out for me to grasp, he was close enough that I could smell him, a combination of his cologne, soap, aftershave, and shampoo. He smelled . . . heavenly. "If we hurry, we can check the pantry for Pop Tarts. Sometimes dietary puts some in there, and the nurses hide them."

"What kind?" I asked, pretending not to be interested as I pulled the robe around my shoulders.

"Strawberry, I think. Do you like strawberry?"

"Strawberry is . . ." I stopped as I noticed his laughing eyes and swallowed. ". . . acceptable."

After the physical therapy session, I felt exhausted. Even still, I couldn't sleep because all I could think of was that pregnancy.

Everybody blaming Matt made it easy for me. The fact that I couldn't abort made me feel panicked. I hated that baby, even when I felt her move inside of me. Every day, I liked hearing the sounds of the infant monitor beeping, speeding up and slowing down, and every day I wished I didn't. With each beep of the monitor, I felt what was left of my sanity going with it.

There were so many things I didn't remember since the accident. I couldn't remember the truck swerving the way they said it did, or the impact of the crash. I didn't remember them pulling me out car with the Jaws of Life. I didn't remember coming to the hospital, or the first several weeks I was there. Why was it the one thing I wished I could forget was burned into my memory like a cattle brand?

That day had started out like all the others. I got up, showered, ate Cheerios, went to school. I saw Emily drive off with Spencer in his sporty little BMW convertible. I had an old red VW Bug, which suited me fine.

I was supposed to spend the night at my friend Andrea's house. We were going go study Biology together, but I got sick. Go figure, the school cafeteria burritos didn't sit well with me. I went home and was going to bed, but I forgot that I took the sheets off my bed to wash them. I had already thrown up once before, and the room spinning so I went to lie down in Emily's room. She always kept her room so neat, and I knew it would be comfortable. The house was quiet, and even the cat was asleep. Mom was working on a trip and Emily was spending the night at her friend Haylee's house as well. I fell into bed, not even bothering to put on pajamas, just took my jeans off before I crashed onto Emily's bed.

Around midnight I heard a noise. I was still so sick, I didn't even pay attention. I figured Emily had forgotten something. I wasn't feeling well enough to give it much though. The door creaked open, then shut quietly. I was about to say something to Emily when I felt somebody slide into bed next to me. Before I could say anything, someone was all over me. His mouth covered mine, the prickles of his beard scratched my chin, and his hands, rough inside my T-shirt, undid my bra. His breath smelled like beer.

I started protesting, but he covered my mouth with one hand and pulled down my panties with the other.

"Isn't this what you like, huh, Emily?"

I heard Spencer's voice, filled with desire and excitement.

"The rape fantasy and all? Oh, wait, I shouldn't talk right now, it will ruin the moment."

Panicked, I jerked my head to break his grip over my mouth. "Spencer! I'm not Emily!" I yelled, then swung blindly at his shadow. The sliced bars of streetlight coming through the blinds provided the only light.

"Oww! What the hell?!" he yelled, and turned on the light.

"Well . . ." He leered. "I'm not happy you tried to hit me, but you do look amazing. How come Emily is the cheerleader? Your body is so much hotter than hers."

Then his lips were on mine as he pushed me back on the bed.

"NO!" I yelled. "Spencer, what are you doing? Leave me alone!"

"Hey!" he said roughly, his breathing heavy. "I came here to get something, and if Emily's not here, you will have to do."

My screaming became muffled when he covered my mouth with his hand. I kept fighting him, but my screaming excited him even more. I tried to push him off, but he was so much bigger and stronger it was futile. I felt myself tear as he forced his way inside of me, but he didn't notice. I screamed again and he laughed. The only merciful thing was how quickly it ended.

He left me there, broken and numb, while he went to the bathroom, whistling.

EDEN

Well, there had been a lot of maneuvering, but we are going to take Sam home today. Frankly, I was worried about it. I wasn't sure she was ready, but she couldn't stay there forever.

Physical therapy had her walking in the halls for several days. Yesterday, I came to see her just as she was heading back to her room. She had a robe on, and fuzzy socks to cover her feet. She was still using a walker for safety, and still moving pretty slowly. She was laughing with the physical therapist, though, and my heart leapt to see her smile. I couldn't remember the last time I saw Sam smile. She took a step forward, and her hospital gown was at just the right angle to show her protruding belly.

I gasped at the sight, then caught myself before Sam could see or hear my reaction. With her up and around, it was very evident that she was pregnant. There was no hiding it anymore. The only good thing was that at least it was summer break and she would be able to deliver the baby before she went back to school. That was the plan anyway.

Craig has been coming to see Eden almost every day. It was so damn hard seeing him. Even after all that we had been through, there was just the tiniest spark left there. A couple of weeks ago when he kissed me, it brought back all those early years of marriage. It was funny how a few years of separation could make it difficult to remember the little things we fought about, but the big things were not so hard to remember.

The night my mother died was also unforgettable. Joy had stood by me, held my hand. Unashamedly I took it, trying to block out the fact that a few weeks prior I had slept with her husband. The hospital staff was not in a flurry that time. Mom was on a ventilator already, and it didn't seem like anybody was really doing anything. In my experience as a nurse, that was when you knew there was trouble. When it seemed like there was nothing left to do. A busy staff running around, yelling orders and spiking bags of fluid meant there was hope.

I heard the doctor talking to the social worker about finding a next of kin, and something about a DNR order.

They explained it to me: Do Not Resuscitate. Evidently, Mom had coded twice during the night, and her system was just too shot to continue. Her vitals were erratic, and her blood pressure was inexplicably dropping to the point where they could barely get a reading. Her brain waves were not registering any activity at all. Apparently the ventilator alone was keeping her alive, for now. She looked dead already.

I heard the doctor talking to Joy in a quiet voice, but not so quiet I didn't glean the fact that he suspected that somebody, one of Mom's loser friends probably, had given her several different kinds of pills. This time the combination had proved to be too much. This time, there was no rescuing her. This time, she had really done it.

Janet, the social worker, motioned me over to a small conference room. She pulled out a chair and motioned that I have a seat. Her serious expression made my stomach tighten. I tried to concentrate on her Prada shoes and matching bag.

"Eden, we need to talk," she said, her kind brown eyes met mine.

"Okay, so talk," I mumbled. I wasn't trying to be rude, I just said the first thing I thought of. A custodian was pushing a dust mop on the shiny tile nearby. I pretended to be very interested in his cleaning.

"I think I found your grandmother. She's here in the waiting room, and she wants to see you," Amy went on. "You are going to go live with her in Arkansas."

"I can't go live with her!" I fumed. "I have to stay here with my mom."

"Eden, I think you know that your mom is not doing very well." Amy bit her lip. She looked reluctant to say the words. "Dr. Franklin thinks she is fading fast. That's one of the reasons we wanted to find your grandmother."

I stared at my shoes. The same black flats I wore the night Bruce and I had slept together. I was really starting to hate those shoes.

Janet walked over and sat next to me. "Eden, I've met your grandmother, Elizabeth. I think she is a nice person, and I think you don't really have a choice about this."

A few minutes later, I saw my grandmother for the first time. Standing next to her was the man I assumed was my grandfather. He had a kind smile and a tear in his eye.

She was petite, like Mama, and pretty, too. She appeared too young to be old enough to be Mama's mother. Her red hair was pulled up in a loose bun, and she wore a simple cotton dress, an emerald green that seemed to match her eyes. I resembled her a lot, I realized. She walked over to me and immediately put her arms around me.

I cried for a long time that day in my grandmother's arms.

Chapter 16

EDEN

After my mother died, my whole world changed. I moved from Tulsa, Oklahoma, to the mountains of Arkansas. Geographically, it wasn't that far, but it seemed light years away. I purposely lost touch with Sarah. I felt like it was best. I knew she didn't understand when I sent her letters back and ignored her calls, and it hurt me, too. But I knew that Bruce didn't want me, and I really did love Joy, and felt bad about what I had done. In some ways, I felt extra guilt, feeling that my fight with Mama had put her over the edge, and caused her to seek out pills to finish herself off. I never shared that with anyone. I viewed moving to War Eagle as a new start.

Living with grandma was a whole new world than what I was used to. Grandma knew how to take care of kids. Even though I was 17 now and not really a kid anymore it was nice to be worried about, instead of the one that was always worrying. It was nice that Grandma cooked meals for us, and knew how to pay her own bills. It was nice not having to be the grown-up. I had never had that before. I'd always had to wash my clothes, and Mama's too. But at Grandma's, she took care of that. She went to the grocery store, and gave me lunch money, and helped me with my homework, and the homework that she couldn't help me with, Grandpa would.

Watching Grandma and Grandpa together was a trip. It was strange seeing two people that loved each other so much and had been together for so long. Not that they didn't have their disagreements, but they usually resolved them quickly and always respectfully. Grandpa listened to Grandma, and if she felt strongly about something he would do what she wanted. There was no yelling or screaming or fighting. There was no drinking or drugs or people over at weird hours. Some people, especially teenagers, might think it was boring to live with Grandma and Grandpa, but I didn't. For the first time ever, I felt safe.

The first day of school was a nightmare. The kids at the high school I went to were not very friendly to me. I was actually looking forward each day to, sadly, Pre-Cal. Math seemed to be the only thing that made sense. I was not interested in boys or activities or anything. Pretty much, I just went to school and came home to see Grandma and Grandpa. They loved me from the start, and did everything they could to make up for the fact that Mama didn't know how to be a mother. I could tell they were worried about me.

When I got to Pre-Cal, I searched for an empty seat in the back of the room. When I sat down, I accidentally dropped my books, making a loud noise, and a bunch of girls laughed at me. When I bent down to pick up the books, I heard his voice. "Here, let me give you a hand with those."

I saw the most beautiful man-boy I had ever seen. He was everything that Bruce wasn't. He was slender and dark and artistic. His hair was kind of in a punk style, and he wore mostly black, but not so much I thought he was Goth. But he did dress well, for a boy, compared to most of the other farmer types in the classroom.

"I'm Craig Langston," he said with a dazzling smile.

I lost my heart right away. We were inseparable the rest of high school, never going anywhere without the other. It made our parents (or in my case, Grandma and Grandpa) worried, and well they should have been. We couldn't keep our hands off each other. There was almost a magnetic force between us. I had to be near him, to touch him, to see him, to hear his voice. If I went too long without him, I literally felt sick. Grandma worried, I know. I knew she was thinking I was acting like my mother, but I wasn't. I didn't do drugs or drink or party or sleep around. I didn't need any of that, because Craig was my drug.

Right after graduation, actually about a month later, we were married. I was accepted into the nursing program at the University of Arkansas. Craig was given a full scholarship by the art department at U of A as well.

He was so talented it was scary. Often times, he'd stay up for days working on a painting. When he went into the artist personality, he was amazing to watch. He would forget everything except his work. The first several times I saw him that way, I was fascinated by him and he seemed to be so focused. He would forget everything barely remembering to go to class, or to eat.

I found that charming, endearing, and damn sexy, especially when he wanted to paint me for a final exam. He insisted it be a nude. I was unconvinced that I was worthy of being an object of a painting, but Craig said he knew better. If I needed convincing, he did so with his passionate lovemaking as he kissed each part of my body and proclaimed me beautiful.

The painting turned out more amazing than anyone, even me, had expected, and I was his biggest fan. When he turned it in, his professor was so impressed he made some calls to some people in the art world that he knew and in days Craig was famous, at least locally. They displayed the painting that he simply called "The Garden of Eden," and it sold for five hundred dollars, which was a lot of money in 1989. That was the second time a man had called me that, and I couldn't help thinking of Bruce when I saw the title of the painting. The old guilt came back in waves, reminding me of how I had nearly destroyed that family with my foolishness.

After that, Craig became too busy to continue going to school, and became more obsessed with his art. I, on the other hand, had to figure out how to do normal, non-artist things like pay the bills and keep food in the house, in addition to trying to keep my grades up to remain in the nursing program. Craig did not have time to deal with the mundane, day-to-day issues of living, like grocery shopping and paying the electric bills. We often had huge fights about this, and we fought like we made love, passionately. We screamed and yelled and insulted each other. The good thing about the fighting was the making up. When we made up, we always made love, or more accurately engaged in hot make-up sex. Sometimes I picked a fight just to get to this result, just to get his attention from his art to me. Sometimes it seemed like he felt like he had painted me, too, and therefore didn't need me anymore. After all, we were only nineteen years old. What did we know about real, lasting love?

When Sam was born, Craig was momentarily in love with her, and he even took a break for a few months to be Mr. Mom for her, so I could get started finding a job myself. Somebody had to bring in regular income to the house, because Craig certainly wasn't. After "The Garden of Eden" sold, he didn't sell anything for quite a while after, almost a year. In the meantime, our bills still had to be paid, and since he would not stoop to get a "crap job" as he put it, I did. I worked at gas stations, then at a local diner earning tips to keep the water turned on so Sam could eat.

When Craig's next few paintings flopped, he became depressed, and severely so. He didn't shower for a week or more, until I physically put him into the shower and turned it on. He'd lost so much weight he'd become a skeleton. Amazingly, because it seemed as if we never had sex anymore, I'd somehow managed to get pregnant again with Emily. As Craig got thinner and thinner, I gained enough weight for the both of us. When Emily was born, he momentarily came out of it for a few weeks, and then, when the newness of having a new baby wore off, he went back to being depressed.

I couldn't take it anymore, and I told him so. "Craig, I'm sorry you're depressed, and I do care about you, but I simply can't raise the girls in this environment. Either get help, or I'm leaving you."

He finally shook himself from his reverie to acknowledge he heard me. He tried valiantly the next few weeks, and I saw a glimmer of hope that he was better for good. He got out of bed, showered, and began painting again. He gained a little weight and got a haircut. He began working again. I got the job at the hospital in the SICU, which I loved, and the girls were growing and thriving. Our little apartment in downtown Fayetteville was nothing great, but it was full of love and had a certain charm. On Friday nights, we'd get a sitter and go down to Dickson Street to dance and listen to the new bands that were trying to make a break into the music business. It was a good life.

Craig started getting excited about his work again, and though he wasn't selling his paintings, he was able to get some work utilizing his artistic gifts with graphic arts. He wasn't as happy designing ads as he was selling paintings, but his pay helped with the rent and the girls were able to go to a private pre-school between his pay and mine. He started to stay up all night again, painting and working, and seemed to be always in a great mood. When he was like that, there was nobody else in the world I wanted to be with. He was fun and loving, and sexy as hell. He wanted to make love all the time, and when the girls were gone, he wanted to make love all over the apartment, and sometimes he wanted to make love in public. One night, we spread a blanket out on the ground in front of the lake and made love under the stars. I wished I could freeze time and keep him like this always.

The bad part about Happy Craig was that he was also Spending Craig. He wanted to pick up the check for all of our friends whenever we went out. He wanted to buy me jewelry I didn't need and we couldn't afford. He would spend large sums of money, often more than what he got paid, on art supplies. His studio, which was basically a breakfast nook in our little apartment, was threatening to take over the whole living space.

Now, all those years later, I realize he probably is bipolar. A lot of really creative people are and his behavior certainly fit the illness.

One night, when the kids were at Grandma Elizabeth's, I got sent home from work early because of low census levels in the hospital (translation: not enough patients). When I came into the apartment, I surprised Craig. He was sitting on a stool and there was a woman, wrapped loosely in a blanket and nothing else, posing for him.

"Eden!" he said, scrambling around, nodding to the woman.

She covered herself and hurried from the room.

"What the hell is going on here?" I asked.

"What the hell is going on here?" I repeated angrily. I could feel the blood rushing toward my cheeks and my heart pounding in my chest.

"Damn, Eden! I'm trying to work here." He rushed after the girl, nearly knocking me over.

I stood there wondering what was happening. Craig was so worried about Julie being offended that he hardly cared that I was upset.

With the both of them gone, I was able to see the painting. Julie was beautiful, it was true. Seeing that perfect body on the canvas made me feel less-than-perfect. I noticed the extra 20 pounds I still had from the pregnancies. I had stretch marks. I felt the tears gathering in the corners of my eyes and told myself I was being silly. Of course, Craig needed to paint more women than just me. I was just being jealous and unreasonable.

"While I hope you're happy, Julie left and I don't know if she's coming back. What's wrong with you?" He ran his fingers through his hair and pinched the bridge of his nose.

"Why didn't you tell me about this project, Craig?" I demanded to know.

"Well, gee, I don't know," he spat, "maybe I thought you would overreact." His blue eyes blazed at me. "I hope you're happy. You probably cost me this project. If I can't get Julie to come back, I'll have to get someone else, which won't be easy, because models talk to each other and if she tells everyone that I have a jealous wife no one will want to work with me."

I felt the tears come rolling down my face. I felt foolish and awkward. I said nothing, but stood there rigidly. He left in a huff, leaving me standing in the doorway with my eyes closed and my fists clenched. That was the beginning of the end for us.

Chapter 17

SAMANTHA

"Excuse me?" I stammered, feeling the slightest edge of panic in my stomach. When I turned to Mrs. Pierson, her eyes went automatically to my bulging belly.

"You heard me, child," she said smoothly, her voice scratchy from years of cigarette smoke. "You're having my son's baby, and I want to know what you're going to do with it," she demanded, plopping down her Prada bag as if it was a grocery sack.

"It's my baby," I said, "and my choice." The minute I said that, I felt remorse. I didn't feel like my baby was an "it." To say it out loud sounded so selfish.

My eyes met hers and I was not the least bit scared. I had my rights, after all.

"I said, what are you planning to do with that baby? If you are giving it up for adoption, I want it. I lost Matt, I'm not going to lose his baby."

That's what happened. That's when I knew: she was mine, no one else's, and Mrs. Pierson was not going to get her hands on her.

A few minutes later Mom stepped in and saw the expression on my face. "Sam, what's going on?"

"Mom, this is Mrs. Pierson, and she seems to think she can have my baby, but she can't." I took a deep breath, realizing importance of my words. "Because I'm keeping her."

Mrs. Pierson took her Prada purse and her expensive shoes out of the hospital room.

Mom and I stood there for a moment. I saw tears pooling in the corners of her eyes. "Sam," she said, "are you sure? I mean, what about Julliard?"

My eyes traveled downward to my swollen belly, and shook my head. "I don't know. I don't have all the answers yet."

"That's okay, baby," I said, holding her in my arms. "We'll figure them out together."

EDEN

We tried to make the marriage work for a couple more months, but it was futile. Craig left quietly one afternoon when I was at work. When I came home, the house felt different. The couch was gone, along with all of Craig's clothes, half of the silverware, half of the plates, and most of the money that had been in the checking account. The funny thing was, I kind of anticipated the money being gone. What I didn't anticipate was how utterly lost I would feel for the next two years.

He didn't try for full custody. The girls went over on the weekends to see him, and a couple of times he would take them along to one of his art shows. They were always excited about that. Over time, his attention seemed to wax and wane, and the girls reacted accordingly. They learned to not take him at his word. Just because he promised to take them to the zoo didn't mean that it was actually going to happen. More than once I felt the need to rip out his heart with my bare hands when I saw one of the girls hurt and disappointed because he "forgot" yet again to do something he promised. When they got older, they just sort of accepted that as par for the course as far as their dad was concerned. It even kind of became part of his charm that he was unreliable: the absent-minded professor syndrome.

But something had changed when Sam went into the hospital. When he said he was coming, he showed. When he said he would take care of something, he did. So that night in the waiting room when he told me he loved me, I believed it. At least for the moment. He made it easy to believe him, when he held me in his arms, and all I could see, hear, smell, taste, was Craig. Even after all those years, he held an attraction for me. Something about the way he moved, talked, even blinked made him not familiar exactly, just easy to be with. The way that stubble grew on his chin when he didn't shave for a couple of days, which seemed out of place compared to the way the immaculately always dressed, the way he would bite his lip when he was nervous, or the way he would absentmindedly picked at his cuticles made him endearing when I was with him. Later, when I was at home, alone again, I was able to think more rationally. I knew what could happen if we got together. It would just end again. We were just too different, with nothing in common anymore.

On the one hand, he was and would always be the girl's father. That could never change. What the problem seemed to be was me. I didn't know if I had the energy or the desire to die all over again when Craig decided he was tired of me, and tired of the family life. And it was really just a matter of time.

Chapter 18

EDEN

When Sam said she was planning to keep the baby, I couldn't believe it. I had so many more questions, like what about high school? Was she planning to graduate? What about Julliard? How was she planning to do this? But one look at Sam's face stopped me in my tracks. It'd been a while since I'd seen that Sam; the strong, determined Sam, who wouldn't let anything get in her way. That was the Sam I had been waiting for, the Sam I had not seen in a while. That was the Sam I knew.

I thought Mrs. Pierson saw that too, even she didn't know Sam. It didn't matter. Sam could be intimidating when she wanted to. And right there in that hospital room, Sam wanted to. Tears welled in my eyes, and thank God Sam didn't see, because it would've made her mad. The tears were there not because I was worried about Sam's future, or the baby, or anything else like that. The tears were there because I just witnessed something amazing. I just witnessed Sam, my oldest daughter, as a mother.

I went home to shower and do a couple of last-minute errands, and to get Sam's prescriptions filled before I picked her up. She had one last physical therapy appointment at the hospital before she was released. When I drove up to the house, I saw Craig sitting on the front porch, smoking, gorgeous as ever. My heart stood still in my chest, and I felt that old familiar pull to him. I tried to check myself, but it was difficult. He was wearing a royal blue shirt that was just unbuttoned enough to show his tanned collarbone. His red tie was loosened a bit, and his dark black slacks and expensive Italian shoes finished the picture. His hair was perfectly groomed, as was the rest of him. In short, he was beautiful.

"Hey, baby." He smiled that slow grin.

"What's up?" I asked. "Are you waiting for Samantha? She won't be home for a while."

"No, actually, I was waiting for you," he said, taking a drag from his cigarette.

"Oh. Okay. Well, do you want to come in?" I found myself saying, then immediately questioned my sanity. What the heck was I doing letting him in? Was I insane? The answer was obviously 'yes'.

He followed me in the door, where Emily was waiting.

"Dad?" she asked, putting down her cell phone. She'd been sitting on the couch texting and watching TV.

"Yeah, sweetie, it's me," he said, kissing her forehead. "Just need to talk to your mom for a few minutes."

"Okay," she said, already distracted by her phone.

We continued past the living room into the kitchen.

"I only have a few minutes. I was going to change clothes and go back to pick up Sam. Did you want to come along?" I asked, wondering if that was it.

"No, I can't. I'm meeting with some people who might want to show my work. It's a very important meeting I can't miss," he said, picking at his cuticles.

Geez, how that got on my nerves. "I see. Did you tell these 'very important people' that your daughter, who almost died a few months ago, is coming home from the hospital today?" I crossed my arms and stared at him.

He rolled his eyes at me. "No, they don't want to hear about my personal life, Eden. You know, you never did understand that aspect of my work. That was one of the issues we had," he said coolly, checking his iPhone that had just dinged.

I pinched the bridge of my nose between my index finger and thumb.

"Do you want to tell me what you want, Craig? I'm in a hurry," I said, getting a glass of water from the fridge.

"Um, okay, well, the thing is . . ." He stalled for a minute, and then seeing my impatience, cut right to the chase. "I wanted to know if I could move back in with you and the girls?" He blurted it out in practically one syllable.

"What?" I said in disbelief. "Why?" I asked, narrowing my eyes.

"Well, it's just that, you know, we've been getting along a lot better, and I figured you might need some help with Sam and the baby, and I don't want to miss anymore of their lives than I already have. I've changed, Eden. I'm ready to be a family man."

SAMANTHA

I finished my physical therapy. I really hated that therapist. Okay, not really, she was pretty nice, but the therapy itself was excruciating.

Some people might think I was crazy to want to keep a baby that was conceived in rape. I was not naïve enough to think it was going to be easy. All I could think about was how it wasn't her fault how she came to be. It wasn't my fault, either. I'm not planning to tell anyone either. Mom said that Emily and Spencer broke up, so at least he wouldn't be coming around the house anymore.

I asked Mom if I could go to another school in town for my senior year. She agreed, probably because she thought I was embarrassed about being pregnant. She probably thought I cared what people thought, but I didn't. I just didn't want to see Spencer again.

That night, after he came out of the bathroom and saw that he had the wrong sister, he didn't even care. He untied me, and I was too much in shock to do or say anything but cry. He actually laughed at me.

"Well, this is not what I expected," he said.

"Spencer, you raped me!" I cried, wild-eyed.

"Well, not exactly . . ." he said, getting a cigarette from his jacket pocket.

"What do you mean, 'not exactly'?" I screamed at him.

"Hey, you wanted me," he said calmly, lighting his cigarette.

"What? Are you delusional? Of course I didn't want you!" My tears stained my kami, and I wrapped myself up in the blanket.

"That's what I'll tell everyone at school if this comes out. That's what I'll tell Emily if you say anything. I'll tell her you tricked me. After all, you were here in her bed, weren't you? How was I to know she wasn't you? Especially when you seduced me in the dark!" He grinned, and the smoke came out his nostrils.

"You wouldn't dare tell people, or Emily, that!" I said, the horror of the night overcoming me.

"Wouldn't I?" he said, finishing his cigarette. "I have a scholarship from Notre Dame that I'm not about to lose for some whore like you."

He came and stood even closer to me. "Even a pretty whore like you. I always thought you were prettier than Emily, but you thought you were too good for a dumb jock like me, didn't you?"

It was true. He did try to ask me out for a few months before he hooked up with Emily. It made her so mad to see him hanging around the house, waiting for me. Emily had thrown herself at Spencer, and I'd told him to leave me alone, I wasn't interested. But he couldn't believe I didn't want to date him. He was the quarterback of the football team. I hadn't said any of that out loud, I just wanted him to leave.

"Remember what I said," Spencer now said as he ground up the butt of his cigarette on Emily's bathroom floor. "She'll never believe a weird band geek like you. Neither will anyone else."

With that, he was gone.

For a week after the rape, I didn't go to school. I said I was sick, which was true. After that, I was too messed up to do anything. Homework seemed pointless, I didn't want to go out with anyone or do anything. Mostly, I just sat in my room and listened to music. Mom noticed something was wrong, but I couldn't tell her. I thought at first she couldn't look at me, because I was acting the way dad did when he couldn't cope with life.

Emily and I barely got along anyway, and that would be too much for our relationship. Besides, I believed Spencer. His dad was on the city council and was rumored to be planning to run for governor the next term. A scandal of that sort would really mess up his chances, which were pretty good. Spencer's family was wealthy and well connected, and I believed him when he said if I told anyone and tried to ruin his life it would backfire on me and ruin my life, not his. The only saving grace I had was that everybody thought Matt was the father, and Matt wasn't around to tell anyone otherwise.

Chapter 19

EMILY

I was excited that Sam was coming home, but there was a problem. There was a big party at Stacy Covington's house that night. I thought that Spencer was probably going to be there. This was my chance to get him back, and I wasn't going to blow it.

I chose my outfit carefully. A layered tank top, mini skirt, perfect shoes, and I even had my hair highlighted a couple of days ago so it looked great. I used my lavender-scented lotion and body spray so I smelled amazing and spent about an hour just on my makeup. When I was done, I had to admit I was hot.

Mom and I had a fight about my being there when Sam got home, but I didn't care. Sam was still on a lot of pain pills anyway, and would probably just go to sleep when she got home. The party was a pool party, and Stacy's parents were going to be out of town. It was my chance, and nobody was getting in my way of getting back with Spencer. That skank that he was with wasn't worth it, and I was going to show him that.

I showed up at the party fashionably late; it had been going on for a few hours. A couple of the jocks that Spencer hung out with were standing on the porch of Stacy's house drinking beer when I showed up. They catcalled at me when they saw me, and I flirted with James for a few minutes, keeping my eyes open for Spencer.

"Wow, Em, you look . . . delicious," Luke Brown, one

of Hunter's friends, said to me. "Can you believe that idiot Spencer dumped a sweet thing like her?"

I went over and sat on James' lap for a second and really played it up. He was delighted with my attention and I could tell he was about to proposition me to go upstairs when I just marched away. I mean, I acted like a skank, but that didn't mean I actually was one. That whole act was for Spencer's benefit. He was standing by the window with his slutty girlfriend, and I could tell seeing me outside with his buddies bothered him.

I went inside the house. There were tons of people, half I didn't know, bumping and grinding to the music. Oh, man, maybe I flirted a little too much with James. He started following me around. How annoying. He brought me a drink, and tried to talk to me but I pretended not to hear him. It was easy, because the music was so loud.

Spencer was talking to his girlfriend, but watching me. I pretended not to notice, and finally gave some attention to poor James. James was delighted with that, and when he saw Spencer coming over, he put his arm around my shoulder. I stiffened but didn't ask him to remove it. It was helping my cause, and I didn't feel bad about using poor James. He obviously just wanted to sleep with me and dump me, just like Spencer did, and I'm not interested in being passed around like a party favor.

Spencer's eyes were on me, and on James. Man, was he drunk. I could smell it on him. The thing about Spencer was, he could hold a lot of liquor. So if he was so drunk I could smell it, he'd been hitting it pretty heavy. I could get drunk from two drinks, so I only sipped the drink James gave me. I had to keep my head.

I faked boredom when Spencer came over. "Hey, Em," he said. "Do you want to go somewhere and talk?"

Before I could say anything, James got in his face. "No, she doesn't, Spencer. You have a date, and Emily is with me."

Okay, I wasn't really, but that was working so I didn't argue.

"What?" Spencer asked, and to my delight, he sounded a little hurt. "Is this true, Emily? Are you with James now?"

I could tell that was making him mad, but, you know, what right did he have to be mad? He'd been hanging all over Jessica earlier. The only reason he even cared was because he thought I had moved on. Of course, James was drunk, too. Let them get in a fight, I didn't care.

"Not really," I admitted. My whole aim of going there was to get him back, not to piss him off.

James gave up easily. Spencer outweighed him by about twenty-five pounds and he didn't like me enough to get his butt kicked. He threw his hands up in the air and left to go get more beer.

"Do you want to talk, Emily?" Spencer asked.

I nodded, and he got a couple of drinks. I followed him up the stairs to one of the empty bedrooms, feeling quite pleased with myself.

We sat on the bed, and he leaned over, putting the drinks on the nightstand.

"What are you doing all the way over there?" he asked, patting the spot next to him.

I moved in closer and we immediately started kissing. I found it hard to ignore the liquor on his breath, it stank so bad, but I was just so glad he wanted me I didn't care. I poured it on strong, pulled him on top of me on the bed, and it didn't take long before we were undressed and all over each other. Before I knew it, we were done.

He stood up right away and started getting dressed.

"Wait, what happened to talking?" I asked, feeling his juices running out of me onto the bedspread.

He laughed. "You don't know how to just talk, Emily. There's only one thing you are good at, and we just did it."

I saw myself, naked and sweaty, in somebody else's house, in somebody else's bedroom, trying to hold on to a guy that didn't even care about me. I had never in my life felt so humiliated as I did in that moment.

"But, wait." I stood up, pathetically reaching for him. He stood over me, tan and beautiful, trying to put his shirt back on. His low-rider jeans fit him perfectly and his muscles rippled as he put one arm into his shirt.

"Stop, Emily," he said, kind of wavering back and forth for a moment. Apparently the alcohol was starting to catch up to him because his speech slurred a bit as well.

"Wait," I said again. "Are we getting back together?" I hated myself and the way I sounded.

"I don't think so," he said, so nonchalant, as if I didn't matter, as if I never mattered. And then he was gone, slamming the door behind him.

I was crying, but it was an angry kind of crying. I sat there for a moment, wondering if I could climb out the window and avoid seeing anyone. Then, as if I woke up from a trance, I got dressed as quickly as possible and made my way down the stairs.

A bunch of people were so freaking drunk it wasn't even funny. A bunch of guys were acting like idiots and doing some kind of really bad white boy dance, and it took a minute to search through the crowd to even be able to tell if Spencer was still here or not. Then I saw him.

He was standing there, with her, as if nothing had happened. He saw me on the stairs, and, after purposely meeting my eyes, he leaned over and started kissing Jessica, right in front of everybody. They started making out so much that they might as well just go right at it in front of everyone. Some of Spencer's buddies started cheering them on, clearly finding the whole thing amusing and probably getting off on the whole thing, when something in me just snapped.

I looked around for something, anything. I found a old softball trophy of Stacy's and pitched it as hard as I could at both of them, aiming at Spencer but not caring really if it hit Jessica or not. My old softball days paid off, and I hit Spencer right in the back of the head.

"What?" he roared, then saw me grinning my angry smile, not even showing my teeth, because they were gritted together. "Bitch!" he yelled, and came toward me.

I took it too far, I thought as he headed toward me. A couple of Spencer's buddies saw what was happening and tried to stop him, but, after all, he was a quarterback and used to being intercepted. He knocked them all out of the way and I tried to run from him, but he grabbed me by the back of my hair.

I cried out, begging him to stop. He roughly spun me around so we were face-to-face. The alcohol reeked in waves with his heavy breathing. His eyes were crazy and wild and red from the booze.

"Nobody does that to me. I ought to rip you apart right here in front of everyone, you little slut," he said through his clenched teeth.

I was cringing and crying, but the more I tried to get away, the harder he held my hair.

James and Luke rushed to him, and James said, "Seriously, Spence, you're hurting her, let her go."

Luke said, "Hey, man, let her go, she's not worth it."

"You're right," Spencer said, pushing me away with a force so hard I fell against the sofa onto a couple of people that were sitting there. "You're not worth it. Your sister was a much better lay, anyway," he said crudely, his speech slurred.

"What?" I whispered in disbelief. "What do you mean, you fucking liar?" I stood up, shaking in fury.

"She at least fought me, and yelled at me to stop, begged, really. It was pathetic. But even then she was a better lay than you. And hotter, too. You would lie down for anyone, even a dog, wouldn't you?" He laughed, poking James' arm, but everyone got really quiet. And Spencer was too wasted to notice.

"Yeah, I heard Sam got knocked up, too." He laughed then went on, seemingly unable to stop, and unaware that everyone was standing there listening to every word.

"The kid's probably mine, for all I know. I told her not to tell anybody. I told her nobody would believe her."

I felt as though my world was spinning. I wondered why everybody was so quiet and what had happened to the music. Then I spotted Stacy's dad and mother standing there, grim and serious.

SAMANTHA

So riding home from the hospital was weird. I hadn't been in a car since the accident, and I was a little jumpy. At one point, I just closed my eyes the rest of the way home because I was so nervous.

The house was the same as always, and I went to the kitchen to get a drink of water. It was kind of late to be getting home from the hospital, but there was a question about some of my take home medications that had to be cleared up before I got discharged, and the doctor couldn't come by to release me to go home until he got out of surgery, which ran late. I was standing in the kitchen drinking a glass of water when the doorbell rang. Mom answered it, and stepped out onto the porch. It was a couple of cops and they were talking to Mom in a quiet voice. She let them in, and in a worried voice, gestured to me.

They stepped into the living room and took off their hats. One of them came over and asked in a kind voice, "Are you Samantha Langston?"

"Yeah," I replied, kind of worried. "Am I in trouble?" I mean, what could I have done? I was in the freaking hospital for the past two and a half months!

"No, you're not in any trouble, but we do need to ask you a few questions," the shorter one said.

Mom interrupted. "You can ask her a few questions, but she just got home from the hospital a few minutes ago and we don't want to upset her too much."

"Don't worry, Mrs. Langston. We're not here to hurt Samantha, we're here to help her."

All of a sudden, I felt as if a fist clenched my stomach, and I felt sick, so sick. I must have looked it because Mom came over and made me sit down.

"Just what is this about, Officer?" she demanded.

Uh, oh, Mama Bear was coming out.

"We just arrested Spencer Blain. He confessed to raping Samantha a few months ago."

Mom immediately started crying.

"That's what we came to ask," the shorter officer said. "See, the boy is quite . . . inebriated, and when he sobers up he's going to deny all of it. Did this happen, Sam? Do you want to press charges?"

Everyone waited for my response. I had trouble forming the words.

"Yes, it happened. Mom, I'm sorry I didn't tell you, I just didn't want to talk about it or think about it, and he threatened me if I told." I could feel the bile come up in my throat.

"And I do want to press charges," I added quietly.

Just then, Emily came in, looking like she'd been run over by a truck. Seeing the cops there, she said, "It's true. Spencer did confess. I was there."

Chapter 20

EDEN

Once everything had come out into the open, Sam seemed a lot better. I saw glimpses of the old Sam coming back now and then and it made me smile. The boy that raped her was being tried as an adult since he was seventeen and a half and rape was considered a felony crime. He was held without bail, and his father's dreams of being governor went up in smoke.

I was washing up some dishes in the kitchen when Sam came in, looking unusually nervous.

"What's wrong, honey?" I asked her, putting the dishtowel on the counter.

"Mom, I need to tell you something. I've needed to tell you for a long time, but I haven't been able to find the words," she said, tears in her eyes.

"What is it, baby?" I went over to her and gave her a hug. I smelled the lavender shampoo in her hair, and as we waited there for a second, I felt the baby kick. We both smiled a little. I've gotten used to the idea of being a grandma, or at least, I've gotten used to the idea of Sam being a mother.

"I know that everyone thinks this baby is Matt's, but it isn't. Matt and I never had sex. I never willingly gave myself to anyone." She was unable to meet my eyes.

I sucked in a breath of air and said nothing. The only sound was the ticking of the clock in the background and the sound of my heart beating, too quickly.

"What are you saying, Sammy?" I asked, using her nickname from when she was six.

Tears filled our eyes. I felt my stomach knot. I held Sam for a long time, and neither of us said anything.

Finally, after a long pause, I said to her, "To me, it doesn't matter. This baby, this life, is half of you. As far as I'm concerned, it's all of you. This baby is ours, our families, and I love her already."

"That's how I feel, too," Sam said. "At first, I didn't know if I could handle it, knowing how she came about. But it's not her fault, and I want her." She fell back into my arms.

I was doing some cleaning around the house when the doorbell rang. I looked like crap, but didn't even care. My hair was in a messy bun, and I was wearing my 'Journey: Live in Concert' shirt and an old ratty pair of cutoffs that were a little too short. Oh well, I was only cleaning the house.

I opened the door and Mike was standing there. He was dressed immaculately, in a red button-up shirt, jeans, and loafers. He held a white bag from the hospital and a grocery bag.

"Oh, hi," I said to him, feeling acutely aware of my grungy appearance.

He seemed not to notice, and broke out in a huge grin when he saw me.

"Hi, Eden, I, uh, hope you don't mind me stopping by. One of the nurses found a couple of Sam's things she forgot in the room that I thought she might want." He handed me the white sack.

"Oh, really? I thought we got everything." I peeked in the sack and all I saw were a pair of hospital socks and an emesis pan. I raised one eyebrow to express my amusement.

"Yeah, you never know when you might need an emesis pan. And those socks are comfortable. Let me tell ya. I got a few pairs back at the house." He smiled mischievously.

I had to laugh at that. I nodded at the other sack, which had the end of a French loaf sticking out the end.

"Oh, I thought you might want dinner, or someone to

cook it, or both." He laughed at his own joke. I couldn't help laughing either. "Sorry to just drop by, but . . ."

"It's okay, come in." I opened the door for him. I pointed the way to the kitchen and he followed me in. I thought to myself, *Man, it's a good thing I just cleaned this up. That moldy meatloaf that I threw away a few minutes ago would probably gross him out.*

He washed his hands and poured some olive oil into a skillet. He was humming to himself, while I stood awkwardly against the countertop.

"Do you want some wine?" I asked him, then wondered if I actually had any.

"I brought some with me, if you want to try it," he said, bringing out a bottle of wine that I couldn't remotely pronounce or that I was the least bit familiar with. With the flair of a magician, he also displayed a cork opener for the wine and opened it. He poured some into a couple of glasses I handed him.

He was expertly sautéing some mushrooms and shrimp when I decided to ask him, "So what made you think about coming over here?" I paused. "And how did you know where I live?"

"Ah, Miss Jeopardy." He smiled. "Okay, why did I think about coming over here? Let's see, maybe that's because I've been trying to get the nerve to come back over here since our date when your ex-husband barged in on us. And then I saw him kissing you, and thought all was lost."

I'd briefly wondered why I hadn't heard from him for a while, and honestly was too busy to put much more thought into it.

"What convinced you that all wasn't lost?" I smiled, taking a sip of my wine.

"Actually, your ex-husband did."

"Craig? What did he do?" I was both intrigued and annoyed.

"Oh, he showed up at the faculty parking lot, and was waiting by my car. Who knows how long he was there. Anyway, when I walked over, he sprang out of nowhere and started asking me about our relationship. He was convinced I was the reason you didn't want him back."

"Ah," I said. "What did you say?"

"I told him to get back on his tiny motorcycle and go home."

"Really?" I giggled.

He turned off the heat and came over next to me. "Really. I wish I could say that I was the reason you didn't want Craig back, but I don't think that highly of myself." He grinned.

He held both of my hands in his. "I haven't stopped thinking about you since we first talked," he said, then he leaned, ever so slowly, in to kiss me.

I hesitated, because it had just been so long since anyone but Craig had kissed me. Mike's lips were soft and gentle on mine, like a feather, and then he took a lock of my hair between his thumb and forefinger. "What do you call this kind of red?"

I didn't know. I could barely think.

"Um, O'Neill red?" I said, smiling. I felt his eyes on my lips, and the yearning behind them. Before I could stop myself, I wrapped my arms around his neck and drew him to me, kissing him until we were both breathless.

"I like it," he said, and began kissing me again, the food forgotten.

SAMANTHA

Emily and I had mended some fences and were even starting to become friends. She knew it wasn't my fault about what happened with Spencer, but I could see it still hurt her sometimes. She still did little things for me here and there, and I did the same. It was hard starting over, but it was necessary.

I wasn't going back to school. I really didn't feel like dealing with the kids there and all their questions. I managed to finish my work from my junior year because all the teachers felt sorry for me, but I couldn't go back there for my senior year. I thought Mom might let me be home-schooled the last year, and she was a great teacher. Then I found an online program as well that would give me an actual diploma. I didn't care so much about the robe and gown and the ceremony.

I planned to also apply to the University of Arkansas for the fall as a music major. I wanted to stay close to home, so Mom and Emily could help with the baby. They'd all promised to do everything they could so I could still go to college. I knew we'd be okay. I asked Mom if we could move to Nana's cabin. She teared up, then said that was a nice idea.

I named the baby Elizabeth Delilah. I knew she would be strong, like us. We are War Eagle Women, after all.